I0531521

Payne has been living with the assassins for four years, and he's finally in a place where he feels he has something to offer. He graduated from high school, and along with Greg, he's a participant in a council program that trains the future council assassins. When he meets his mate, he thinks his life is as perfect as it could be.

Until his mate rejects him.

Rob moved in with the assassins to help Jasper. At first, he doesn't understand what Payne means when he says they're mates—it's just not possible. Payne is young and handsome, while Rob has always been more focused on his work than his personal life. He feels there's been a mistake and that he can never be good enough for Payne.

What if Payne feels the same?

Payne and Rob both feel they're not good enough for the other, but they're mates, and nothing can change that. Can they get over their insecurities and find their way to each other? Or will they think they know better than fate itself?

The unauthorized reproduction or distribution of this copyrighted work is illegal. Criminal copyright infringement, including infringement without monetary gain, is investigated by the FBI and is punishable by up to 5 years in federal prison and a fine of $250,000.

This book is a work of fiction. Names, characters, places, and incidents either are products of the author's imagination or are used fictitiously. Any resemblance to actual events or locales or persons, living or dead, is entirely coincidental.

Payne
Copyright © 2022 Catherine Lievens
ISBN: 978-1-4874-3638-4
Cover art by Angela Waters

All rights reserved. Except for use in any review, the reproduction or utilization of this work in whole or in part in any form by any electronic, mechanical or other means, now known or hereafter invented, is forbidden without the written permission of the publisher.

Published by eXtasy Books Inc

Look for us online at:
www.eXtasybooks.com

Payne
Council Assassins 15

By

Catherine Lievens

CHAPTER ONE

Payne pushed Gregory. He'd pushed too hard, and his friend almost fell off Payne's bed. He continued laughing, and Payne laughed with him.

"I don't want you and your boyfriend to talk about me," Payne warned, pointing his finger at his best friend.

"We're just worried," Gregory said. He was still snickering.

"There's nothing to be worried about."

"Isn't there? Have you decided what you want to do next, then?"

Payne resisted the urge to stick his tongue out. They weren't children anymore. To be fair, they hadn't been children in a long time, even when they were young.

He sighed heavily and flopped back onto the bed. "I don't know. I know what I want to do, but I'm not sure I'll be allowed to."

Greg stretched out next to him, staring at the ceiling. "Yeah, I understand that. We're going to have to do something, though. We can't just sit around."

Payne agreed. The assassins had welcomed them when they needed a place to call home, a place where they could feel safe, and Payne would always be grateful for that. Without the assassins, he and Greg wouldn't have had the opportunity to go to school or have a family. Payne wanted to repay them in some way, but how?

For the past few years, the assassins had been his entire world. He didn't have anything beyond them, and while he didn't care about that, it didn't make it easier to decide what he wanted to do with his life. He was twenty now, and he'd graduated from high school. It had taken him a while because of all the time he'd lost when he'd been sold to the human, but he was finally done.

And now, he had no idea what to do.

His phone vibrated in his pocket. He wiggled until he managed to get it out and stared at the screen, squinting when he saw the name on it.

"Win just texted me."

"He just texted me, too," Greg said. He sounded puzzled.

Payne shared that feeling. Win was the assassins' handler, which meant Payne and Greg didn't have anything to do with him very often, especially not in a professional capacity. They saw him at meals and around the warehouse, but that was that. They weren't assassins, so they didn't need much from him, and he didn't need anything from them.

Except that maybe he did.

Payne sat up and raked a hand through his hair. "Why does he want to see me in his office?"

"Us, you mean," Greg said. He twisted his phone around so Payne could see the text there.

It was the same one he'd just received.

"All right. Why does he need to see both of us, then?" Payne's stomach turned. "You don't think he's going to kick us out because we're not contributing, right?"

"Why would he kick us out? This is our home."

"Well, yeah. But we're supposed to contribute, aren't we? Everyone does, even the mates."

"And we don't do anything now that we're done with school."

"I'm sure he wouldn't dare kick *you* out." Because Greg was mated to one of the assassins, Evan. If Win did something that displeased Evan, Evan would leave, and the council would have one fewer assassin.

But Payne? He didn't have anyone here. He had Greg, who was his best friend, and Evan, who felt a bit like a brother-in-law. He had Armand, who'd taken on the role of adoptive father, even though Payne had already been sixteen when he found him. Armand was protective, so Payne doubted he'd allow Win to kick him out, but still.

Payne didn't want to start a war between the assassins, and he was sure that if Win was kicking him out, he had a good reason to do so. Knowing that didn't make things easier.

Greg climbed off the bed. "Well, whatever he wants, we should head there and find out."

He wasn't as scared as Payne, and it made sense. Greg was more secure in his position with the assassins because of Evan. He knew that Evan would have his back whatever happened, and not for the first time, Payne wished he'd meet his mate.

Only to hope he wouldn't meet them seconds later.

None of the assassins was his mate. After living in the same house as them for four years, he was sure of that. That meant that if he found his mate, it would be someone outside of their family. That was probably a good thing, but it would mean that Payne would have to leave, and he didn't want to. He realized that eventually he'd have to live his life and not continue hiding here, but he wasn't ready to do so yet.

He wanted to be an assassin, since he and Greg had arrived at the warehouse. He'd been watching the assassins, and he trained with them, but none of that changed the fact that he was just a regular shifter. The council assassins were anything but regular. Each of them had a special ability that had been forced on them in a lab, and while Payne's life hadn't been easy, nothing like that happened to him. No matter how much he wished for it when he first arrived, he was still just a fennec fox shifter — nothing more, nothing less.

Greg was staring at him expectantly, so Payne slid off the bed. He tried delaying by stretching, then looking around for his shoes, but Greg pushed him toward the door. "Stop that."

"I'm not doing anything," Payne protested.

"That's bullshit. You're wasting time, and I know it's because you're afraid Win will kick you out. He's not going to, so stop worrying about it."

Payne found one of his shoes and pushed his foot into it. "That's easy for you to say. You know you're not going anywhere because of Evan."

"And you're not going anywhere because these people are family. Maybe Win wants to have a chat with us now that we're done with school. I think it makes sense, and I'm not opposed to it. Who better than him to help us find out what we want to do next?"

Payne supposed Greg was right, but he was still anxious as they headed downstairs. They walked by the kitchen and stopped to get a snack, but they were out of excuses by the time they were done eating. Well, Payne was. For some reason, Greg looked excited about whatever Win was about to tell them. Payne wished he could feel the same, but instead, it took everything he had not to turn around and run.

Greg seemed to realize that, because he quickly knocked on the office door they were standing in front of. He stared at Payne for a moment, possibly trying to make him understand without saying anything—that no matter what happened—they'd always be best friends. That was the kind of person Greg was. He was more worried about Payne than about what was about to happen to him.

"Come in," Win's voice called out from inside.

Greg pushed open the door and peeked in. His eyes widened, and Payne understood why when he followed him inside and saw that Roark was there, too. Whatever they were about to be told, it had to be important.

"Sit down," Win said, waving at the chairs on the other side of his desk.

Roark was already in one of them, but it left two of them empty. Payne gingerly sat on the edge of one, his gaze bouncing from Win to Roark.

Why were they both here? They worked together and were responsible for the assassins, but usually, each of them had their own job. It didn't make sense that they were working together now, especially not when it involved Greg and Payne.

"I'll get straight to the point," Win said as he linked his fingers together on top of his desk. "I'm proud of you."

Payne blinked. It wasn't what he'd expected. "Thank you," he said.

Win grinned. "But you're still wondering why you're here. Well, I know both of you have finished high school recently. That's what I was referring to when I said I was proud of you, among other things. Over the past four years, you've shown us that we were right to give you a chance and welcome you into our home. We've never regretted it, and I want to give you an opportunity that just arose."

Payne leaned forward. *An opportunity?* That sounded interesting.

"With everything that's happening, between the government still working in those labs and some of us retiring or thinking about doing so, the council realized that they'll need more assassins. They found and trained us one by one the first time around, and it took them a while. Now they already have our team in place, and they're willing to try another approach. They've created a camp, if you will. There, they'll train the next generation of council assassins."

"That sounds interesting, but I'm not sure what it has to do with us," Payne pointed out.

"They're recruiting, and they reached out to me to ask if I

had anyone in mind. I gave them both your names."

"But we don't have special abilities," Greg said.

Payne glared at him, even though it wasn't like Win would have forgotten.

"And they don't care about that," Win answered. "They want you to give this program a try because you've been living with us for four years. You know this life. You know how dangerous it is and what the council will expect of you. You don't have to say yes right away, but you should think about it. If you've ever wanted to become an assassin, this is your chance."

It took everything Payne had not to scream that he was in right away. Win was right. This was an opportunity he'd never thought he'd have, and while he knew what he wanted to do, he wouldn't do it alone. Since the beginning, he and Greg had been in this together, and Payne wanted that to continue.

Rob's eyes burned. He blinked and realized that it was worse with the right one. It almost felt like something was stuck in there, and he rubbed it, trying to dislodge whatever it was.

It was even worse when he stopped rubbing.

He groaned and closed his eyes for a moment, relaxing in relief. How long had he been working on his computer? If the state of his eyes was anything to go by, probably too long. He wasn't hungry, but he usually wasn't, especially when he was working. He had to remind himself that he needed to eat, and he often forgot.

He tried to remember the last time he'd eaten something, and since he was sure he remembered some toast and coffee earlier this morning, he decided he was good. He could work for a while longer, then go to lunch.

He rubbed his eyes again, swore when he opened them and

they burned, but he turned his attention back to his computer.

"Okay, this is it," a voice said.

Rob blinked again. "I didn't hear you come in," he said, turning his chair around to face his friend.

Rocco stood behind him, his hands on his hips. He stared at Rob for a moment, then sighed. "I'm not surprised. You look like shit."

"Why, thank you. I don't know what I'd do if it weren't for your compliments."

Rocco rolled his eyes. "At least you're still snarky. That has to mean it's not that bad yet, right?"

"What are you talking about?"

"When was the last time you ate?"

"I had toast and coffee this morning."

Rocco stared for a moment. Rob didn't understand why he was looking at him like that, but it made him uneasy, and he wiggled in his chair.

"Rob, that was yesterday morning."

Rob frowned. "That's not possible. I'd be hungry if I'd not eaten since yesterday morning."

"Maybe, maybe not. I promise that it was yesterday morning, though. You weren't at breakfast today. Did you even go to bed last night?"

Rob didn't want to lie to Rocco, so instead, he stared at him.

Rocco sighed and rubbed his forehead. "Probably not, considering you're wearing the same clothes you wore yesterday."

Rob looked down at himself. He was wearing a white shirt that was all wrinkled and looked like it might stand by itself if he took it off. Luckily, his white coat hid most of it, and he wrapped it tighter around his torso to hide the shirt. His dress pants looked fine, although he couldn't remember when he'd put them on.

"You're going to work yourself into an early grave," Rocco

said. He leaned his hip against the desk and crossed his arms over his chest.

Rob disliked having people look down at him, but this was Rocco. They'd been friends for a few years now, even though they rarely saw each other.

That had changed when Rocco had asked Rob to come to help him. Rob hadn't been sure whether to say yes, but when Rocco had told him what happened to Jasper, he'd known he couldn't abandon the man. Rob was human and could never understand how Jasper felt about what had been done to him, but he could do his best to help him fix things.

Although there was no fixing the fact that Jasper wasn't entirely human anymore.

"You're not going to help Jasper by not eating or sleeping," Rocco said.

"It wasn't my intention." Now that he knew it had been an entire day since he'd last eaten, Rob felt it. He wanted nothing more than to faceplant in his bed, possibly after eating something.

His gaze strayed to his computer. There was so much work to do. He was still going over the data and files the scientists had gathered on Jasper. They'd been thorough, even though Rocco hadn't realized it in the beginning. He was a doctor, and he'd been looking for an easy solution. There was no easy solution in Jasper's case. He'd never go back to what he'd been before, and Rob doubted they could change anything about his situation right now. The only thing he could do was find out exactly what had been done to him and help him live with that as best he could.

"I know," Rocco said. He sounded understanding. "But since you've been here for the past twenty-four hours, it's time to take a step away from your computer."

"I still have a lot of work to do."

"I'm aware of that. Work never ends, but your involvement

in it can."

Rob's eyes widened, and he shot to his feet. "You wouldn't dare."

Rocco arched a brow. "Are you willing to try me and see what happens? I still think you're the best person to help Jasper and that I was right to call you, but I won't have a hand in your self-destruction."

"I'm not doing any of this on purpose," Rob said as he stepped back and raked a hand through his hair. He winced when his fingers got caught. His hair was tangled and oily, and it was frankly disgusting.

"I never said you were. I know you're trying to help Jasper and that all of this is extremely interesting to you, but you need food, sleep, and a shower."

Rocco didn't say that Rob stank, but Rob suspected he did.

He also suspected that he knew what would happen if he continued pushing himself. He'd done it a time or two, but he usually didn't have anyone who tried to stop him from over-working. He mainly worked on his own, and he typically realized it was time to take a break only when he was about to faint.

He couldn't afford to get sick. The last time that happened, he'd wasted days getting better.

"Fine. I'll do all of those things."

Rocco kept an eye on him as he turned back to his computer, saved his work, and powered it down. Once he had, he turned to glare at his friend. "Happy?"

"Very much so. Let's go to the kitchen."

Rob had expected to go to his room, sleep, shower, and only then get food. He wasn't really hungry, so food could wait. He could tell from Rocco's expression that his friend wouldn't allow him to do that, though, so with a sigh, he followed him toward the door.

"You realize I'm an adult, right?" Rob asked as they

stepped into the hallway.

He blinked at the harshness of the lights. His eyes needed a break, and now that he'd stepped away from his computer, he couldn't wait to sleep for at least twelve hours.

"Really? Because from where I stand, you're behaving like a teenager."

"That's not true. If I were behaving like a teenager, I'd be on my phone all the time, and I wouldn't listen to you."

Rocco shook his head, but he was smiling. "True. It reminds me of when Payne and Gregory had just arrived here."

Rob tried to remember who he was talking about, but he couldn't place the names. He was sure he'd met them, but he'd spent most of his time in the infirmary since he'd arrived. The only person he saw regularly was Rocco and sometimes Jasper. Jasper's mate was also there when he and Jasper talked, but that was about it.

Rob had never done great in social situations, which was why he hadn't been bothered by the fact that he spent most of his time alone in the infirmary. It looked like Rocco was dragging him to the kitchen, though, which probably meant he was about to meet some of the people Rocco lived with.

Rob didn't understand that. How could Rocco share living spaces with so many people? It would drive Rob nuts, although he had to admit that he wasn't dying to go back home, unlike what he'd thought in the beginning. That probably had more to do with his work than with this place, but still. He wasn't so uncomfortable that he wanted nothing more than to run away, which in his mind, was a victory.

"You know, you're not going to solve all of Jasper's problems in one day," Rocco said. "And you definitely won't solve any of them if you work yourself into an early grave."

Rob groaned. "You already said that, and I agreed. There's no need for you to repeat yourself."

"I don't know about that. I'm glad you decided to step

away from your computer for now, though."

"I don't think I had a choice," Rob snarked.

Rocco didn't care. He grinned, obviously happy to have gotten Rob away from the infirmary. "That's fine. If I'd known this was what I needed to do, I'd have done it sooner."

Rob didn't doubt that his friend was telling the truth. If he didn't want Rocco to interrupt his work, he supposed he would have to remember to eat, sleep, and shower regularly.

Easier said than done.

Both Payne and Greg were silent for a moment after they left Win's office. Then they both started talking at the same time.

"What do you think about it?" Payne asked.

"Isn't it great?"

They stared at each other. Then they started laughing.

"I just can't believe it," Payne said.

"Well, believe it, because it looks like we're going to become council assassins."

"You've already decided to accept, then?" Payne didn't want to do it alone. He wanted his best friend by his side and for them to do it together.

"Well, I'll have to talk to Evan first. He'll want to know about it, but he won't forbid me to do it."

"But if he's not okay with it, you won't do it."

Greg grimaced. "I don't want to do anything that would hurt him, and to be honest, if he said no, I'd understand. It's not going to be easy, and it *will* be dangerous."

"He goes on missions all the time." Although since he and Greg had gotten together, it wasn't as often as before.

"Yeah, but he has his ability. You and I are just normal shifters."

"Win wouldn't have asked us to do this if he didn't think we could."

"I agree, but I don't have just myself to think about, Payne. Evan is important to me, as is our life together. We don't make big decisions without talking to the other."

Payne understood, and he didn't berate Greg for wanting to talk to his mate first. Evan wasn't just a boyfriend, but it would be his right to know what was happening and to have a say in it, even if he had been. He and Greg were mates, which was even more important. "Well, I hope he'll say yes."

"I told you, he won't forbid me from doing anything."

"But he can look at you with those sad eyes of his and convince you not to."

Greg laughed. "That much is true."

"That's why I'm better on my own."

Greg clapped Payne's back. "Wait until you find your mate. I'll be here, laughing at you."

"I doubt I'll find them anytime soon. What are the odds? Besides, I barely leave the house."

"But we'll be leaving the house to go to this camp. Maybe your mate will be one of the other trainees."

If Payne was honest, the thought of leaving the warehouse made him nervous. It had become his home over the past four years and the only place where he felt safe. It made sense after what had happened to him when he was a child, but he realized it wasn't healthy for him to spend all his time here. Being part of this program would force him to step out of his comfort zone, and while he was eager to start working and training, he was also a little scared. What if he sucked? What if Greg became a great assassin, and Payne didn't? He'd never lose his friend, but he'd been thinking about becoming an assassin since he'd moved in with them, and he didn't have a plan B. He didn't know what he'd do if he couldn't do this.

Greg grabbed Payne's shoulder and squeezed. "You'll be great," he said.

He sounded convinced, and he probably was. Payne

wished he could have the same faith in himself as Greg had in him.

But he was excited about the opportunity. He couldn't focus on what might happen, especially before getting there. If he couldn't do it, he'd find something else.

He just hoped he wouldn't have to.

"I'm hungry," he declared, ready to stop thinking about how bad he would be as an assassin.

Greg snickered. "Aren't you always hungry?"

"I'm not the only one."

"True. Let's go to the kitchen. I'm sure Graham has some snacks ready."

Payne was glad that he and Greg would be allowed to stay with the assassins even as they went through the program. It would be a big step for him to leave the warehouse, and he wasn't sure how he'd have reacted if he'd had to share living spaces with the other trainees. Win had told them it was a possibility if they wanted to but that they'd be allowed to stay back because of their particular circumstances. It was good to know they'd be coming home to their family once training was over. Payne suspected that the other trainees might have something to say about that, but he didn't care. He couldn't stop thinking about what his future would be like once he became an assassin, and the feeling carried him all the way to the kitchen.

Like always, the room was crowded. Graham was in front of the stove, working on lunch. Evan was sitting on the couch, but he looked up as soon as Greg walked into the room, as if he'd been able to feel him. They were both shifters, so they couldn't talk in each other's minds as Nix could, which meant that wasn't the right explanation. Payne didn't have another one, and honestly, he didn't care. As long as Greg was happy, he and Evan could do whatever they wanted.

Armand was sitting at the counter, scrolling on his phone,

but he put it away when Payne entered. He grinned at him and patted the stool next to his, and Payne didn't hesitate.

He had a strange relationship with Armand. The man wasn't old enough to be Payne's father, but he'd taken on that role after they'd first met, even though Payne hadn't asked him to. He'd protected him and had talked Win into letting him and Greg stay. Of course, the fact that Evan was Greg's mate had probably helped, but it would have been easy for Win and the others to dump Payne somewhere and never think about him again. But Armand had taken him under his wing, and to this day, they were close.

"I heard that you and Greg were called to Win's office," Armand said.

Payne rolled his eyes. Nothing ever stayed a secret for long in this place. "And you want to know what happened?"

"Of course I do. What did you do?"

"For once, nothing."

Armand's expression changed. "Not for once. You're a good kid."

"Not a kid anymore," Payne pointed out.

"For me, you'll always be a kid, and besides, you're only twenty. So, what did Win want?"

Payne looked up to see that Greg and Evan were quietly talking in a corner. He had no doubt that Greg was telling his mate about the offer, and to be honest, he wanted to shout it from the rooftops.

He still couldn't believe that Win and Roark agreed that he had potential. Most days, he wasn't sure about it, yet *they* believed in him. It was humbling, and he promised himself that if he ended up in the program, he'd do whatever he had to in order to make them proud.

"Payne?"

Payne grinned. "Apparently, there's a program for new council assassins. People are going to train them, things like that, and Win wants me and Greg to be part of it."

"That's great!"

Armand knew how important this was to Payne, and his reaction made Payne smile. "It is. I can hardly believe it. Win chose both of us to be part of this program, which means we're going to become council assassins."

"I won't deny that I'm a bit worried, but I know how much this means to you, and if you're happy, I'm happy."

Armand gave Payne a sideways hug, and Payne leaned back against him. He straightened just as the door opened again, and Rocco walked in with his scientist friend.

Payne was intrigued by the man, but they'd never talked. He'd barely seen him, actually. Rob didn't usually eat his meals with the others, and he was a bit of a mystery. He spent most of his time in the infirmary, and Payne didn't want to visit him there because he didn't want to bother him. Besides, the way he felt drawn to the man was odd, and he wasn't entirely comfortable with it. It was better to ignore it and focus on the great news he'd just gotten.

But just as Rob and Rocco walked past the counter where Payne was sitting, Armand gave Payne a little shove. He tilted sideways, and even though he tried to grab the counter to keep himself up, it wasn't enough. He hit Rob, who scrambled to keep both of them upright.

It was then that Payne's face ended up smashed against Rob's chest. It was hard, a bit bony, but that wasn't what Payne cared about. No, what he cared about was the scent that came from Rob.

It hit Payne like a train. His fox sat up in the back of his mind, grinning like an idiot at the thought that they'd found their mate.

Rob had no idea what was happening, but he didn't want the

pretty man to hit the floor, so he kept his hold on him. The man was frozen, but it only lasted for a second. Then he scrambled back onto the stool, staring at Rob with wide eyes. "You're my mate," he blurted out.

Everyone in the room stopped talking. Rob stared at the man. He'd heard what the man said, but it was as if his brain couldn't understand the words. There was no way that this gorgeous young man was destined to be with Rob.

Was there?

"Payne?" the older man sitting next to Payne asked. He sounded worried, a feeling Rob agreed with.

Payne—possibly Rob's mate, possibly not—blinked. "I'm not kidding," he said.

"I never said you were, but you look in shock."

Payne snorted. "That's because I am."

He was in shock? What about Rob? Rob was human, and he wasn't supposed to have a mate. He didn't know what to *do* with a mate. Maybe if Payne had been closer to his age and had shared his interests, Rob could have done something about it. As it was, he didn't see how anything could be possible between them.

He cleared his throat. "Could you possibly repeat what you just said?"

"You heard me. I said we were mates, and I meant it. I can smell it."

"But that's not possible."

Payne jerked back as if Rob had hit him.

Rob instantly felt sorry, but when he found himself reaching for Payne without even thinking about it, Payne scrambled off his stool.

"I realize I'm probably not what you expected or wanted, but there's no mistake," he said. "You're my mate."

Rob opened his mouth, although he wasn't sure what he was about to say. He didn't have to say anything, because

Payne turned around and rushed to the door. He disappeared in seconds, leaving Rob standing there, looking like an idiot.

"How could you do something like that to him?" the man who'd been sitting next to Payne asked.

Rob frowned, trying to remember his name. If he remembered right, it sounded kind of French. "Do what?" he asked.

"You rejected him," Rocco said. He pressed a hand against Rob's back as if to reassure him.

"I didn't reject him! I just said it was impossible. You have to see that's the truth."

The French-named man crossed his arms over his chest and glared. "Why wouldn't it be possible?"

"You saw him, and you can see me. Who in their right mind would put us together?"

"You think you're too good for Payne?"

Was the man an idiot? "I'm sorry, François, but that's not what I was saying."

The man stared. "Who's François?"

Rob waved his words away. "Or whatever your name is. I don't remember it."

"My name is *Armand*, and you're going to remember it because I'm about to kick your ass."

Thankfully, Rocco put himself between Rob and Armand. "You need to hear what he has to say," he told Armand. "Rob has never said he didn't want Payne."

"Saying he doesn't think it's possible points to the fact that he doesn't," Armand argued.

How could these people not see what was obvious? "What I meant when I said that this was impossible is that Payne and I are obviously too different. You asked if I thought he wasn't good enough for me, but if anything, it's obvious *I'm* not good enough for *him*. He's young, beautiful, and has all his life in front of him. Me? I'm an odd little man in his late thirties who barely leaves his lab. How could things work between us?"

17

Rob looked at Rocco. "Are we sure that wasn't a mistake?"

"You'd have to ask Payne, but I doubt it. When a shifter meets their mate, they know. It's in the scent."

Rob carefully pulled his shirt away from his torso and sniffed it. It didn't smell great, but it was clear that his stench had a different meaning for him than it did for Payne.

"You're not going to understand, not entirely," Rocco explained. "You're human. To you, you just smell like yourself. That's not the case for Payne. As soon as he was close enough to you, both he and his fox knew they'd found you."

"But that doesn't make sense," Rob protested.

"I agree," Armand said.

Rob hadn't expected it. "You do?"

"Payne doesn't deserve such an asshole as his mate."

Rob sighed. He wasn't angry at being called an asshole. After all, he'd hurt Payne. He hadn't meant to, but this was a social situation—one he'd never been in, to boot. He had no idea how to react or what to say, and in these situations, he usually ended up making a mess. That was why he was more comfortable never leaving his lab, and he wouldn't have if Rocco hadn't needed his help. As it was, he was tempted to return home and never leave it again.

"Stop it," Rocco ordered Armand. "You don't know Rob, so you don't get to judge him or call him an asshole. He was surprised, and as a human, he doesn't fully understand what this means."

"That's bullshit. Humans have known about us for years. He has to be aware of what it means for Payne."

Rob was getting a headache. He'd known leaving the infirmary was a bad idea, and he wondered if anyone would try to stop him if he tried running back there and locking himself in.

"I'm sure he does know something about being mates, but he sucks at being with people. I'm not talking just shifters, either. He sucks at being with people in general. He doesn't believe in not asking questions or not saying what's on his mind."

Rob rubbed his face. That much was true, but he understood how wrong he'd been in this situation. "I was in shock," he explained, hoping these people would forgive him. He didn't really care what they thought about him, but they mattered to Rocco. "I still am, to be honest."

"Don't you remember when you met your mate?" Rocco asked Armand. "Things are always more complicated than we expect or want them to be."

Armand looked like he wanted to disagree, but he begrudgingly didn't. "Fine. I can admit that meeting your mate isn't usually an easy thing to deal with." He pointed his finger at Rob. "But you have to talk to Payne and explain why you reacted the way you did. I know him, so I'm sure he's beating himself up for not being good enough for you right now. If *I* thought that was what you were saying, then he did, too, and it's not fair to him to continue believing that."

Rob raised his hands. "I have no problems talking to him."

"Good."

But it wasn't. Rob had no idea what to do with any of this. He needed to focus on his work and Jasper, but instead, he found himself wondering if Payne was crying right now. Maybe he should try to find him and apologize right away.

Rob softly snorted. He'd probably make things even worse.

"Everything okay?" Rocco asked.

"Honestly, I have no idea. I didn't expect any of this to happen when I agreed to come here."

Rocco's smile was gentle. "I doubt anyone could have expected it. You realize you don't have to be with Payne if you don't want to, right?"

Rob frowned. "But we're supposed to be together." Even though it didn't make one lick of sense.

"Not *supposed*. I guess that, in theory, you and Payne are perfect for each other. It doesn't mean you should be together."

Rob had never heard anything so ridiculous. How could he and Payne be perfect for each other when they were so different? "There has to be a mistake."

"There are no mistakes when it comes to mates, Rob. You and Payne need to talk as soon as possible."

That was one thing Rob agreed on. He didn't want to make Payne sad, but he also knew that there was no way the two of them could be destined to be together. Payne had to have made a mistake, and Rob was sure that once he talked to him, Payne would realize it, and everything would be okay.

It had to be.

CHAPTER TWO

"So, what do you think it's going to be like?" Greg asked.

Payne forced himself to think about what Greg was asking rather than about Rob. "There will be a lot of training."

"That goes without saying. I want to know what kind of training they're going to put us through, though. Who will the instructors be? I doubt they'll be retired assassins, although I suppose it's possible. Has anyone here mentioned it?"

Payne shook his head. "No, but then, the assassins here aren't retired except for Rocco and Roark. They both already have a job, so I don't see why they would go for this."

Greg nodded. He was basically bouncing on Payne's bed, and while Payne would have shared his enthusiasm yesterday, today, he wasn't sure how to feel.

He was still excited about the opportunity of learning to be a council assassin. He'd go through the program, and he'd be working with Armand and the others when he came out of it. But that wasn't what he was thinking about right now, even though he'd waited for this opportunity for years.

Right now, his thoughts were focused on Rob, and he didn't know how to stop it. He wasn't even sure he could, because his thoughts drifted back to Rob every time he tried to think about something else.

"We should ask the others about the retired assassins," Greg said. "They'll probably know them."

"Unless they didn't work at the same time," Payne pointed out. "We can try, though. Has Evan told you anything?"

"Not really, but he's one of the youngest here, so it makes sense that he doesn't know many of the retired assassins. We should ask Roark or someone who's been here a while."

"We can do that. What does Evan think of this opportunity, then? Have the two of you talked about it?" Payne knew they had, and it was easier to focus on Greg and Evan than on Rob.

Greg's smile softened. "We did. He's glad I found something I want to do with my life, and he supports me."

"Well, that's not a surprise. We always knew he'd support you."

Greg nodded. "He's a bit worried, and I don't blame him, but I pointed out that it's going to be a while before either of us is allowed to work as an assassin. They won't want to risk us before we're ready, and while Win didn't mention how long the program will last, I wouldn't be surprised if it's more than a year."

"Probably." And it felt good to know that for the next year or so, Payne knew what he'd be doing with his life. He could focus on what was next once that was over. In the meantime, he'd be busy. Hopefully, busy enough not to obsess over Rob.

"What about you?" Greg asked.

From the tone of his voice, Payne knew what his friend was asking. He didn't want to answer, and Greg would let it go if he said so, but maybe it would be good for him to talk about it. Maybe that was what he needed to forget Rob. "What about me?"

Greg's eyes narrowed. "You know what I'm asking. Have you talked to Rob? What does he think about this opportunity?"

"I wouldn't know. I haven't seen him since the kitchen." Payne didn't have to say when that was, because it was impossible for anyone to forget.

Greg had been there to see Payne's humiliation, and it hurt. At the same time, Payne was glad he hadn't been alone. His friend knew what he'd gone through, and he was here for him.

"Shouldn't you at least try talking to him? I know it's tempting to avoid him for the rest of your life, considering what happened between the two of you, but I think it would be better for both of you to talk things out."

He was right. At the very least, Rob could reject Payne to his face. Not that he hadn't the first time around. He'd been stunned and kept saying that it was impossible that the two of them were mates. Obviously, he thought Payne wouldn't fit in his life, and Payne couldn't say he was wrong. What did they have in common?

Payne was only twenty. He'd finished high school late because of what happened to him as a child and teenager, and even though he had prospects for a job now, it would take a while before he was done with all the training and studying. In the meantime, he still lived here, with everyone else. It wasn't exactly like living with their parents, although it felt like it some days.

But Rob? He was a full-blown adult. Payne wasn't sure how old he was, but he had to be in his thirties, at the very least. He was super smart, and he probably had two or three degrees. He was helping Jasper and trying to make Jasper's life better and easier, and he did things Payne couldn't even begin to wrap his mind around.

How could they make that work?

Payne wasn't sure they could, but he would have been up to trying if Rob was. Clearly, he wasn't, and Payne had decided it would be better for him to stay away. It would hurt less, and it would give both of them time to wrap their minds around what had happened and accept that something had gone wrong.

"Payne?" Greg gently prodded.

"I just don't get it," Payne blurted out. "You know him.

He's older, smarter, and gorgeous. He's infinitely more successful than I can ever be. How did he end up being my mate?"

"Don't say that as if you're not a catch, because that's not the case," Greg warned.

"You say that because you're my best friend. Of course you think I'm great. Rob didn't, though."

"Look, I don't know Rob well. I don't think anyone but Rocco does, which makes sense, considering why he's here. But I don't think you should assume anything before you talk to him. Yes, maybe he doesn't believe the two of you fit together, but you can't know that for sure until you talk to him. Maybe he was just shocked at the thought of having a mate. He's human, and from what I gathered, he spends more time working than living his life. I'll eat my shoe if he's had a boyfriend in the past year."

"What do you know?" Greg had to know something to talk about Rob that way.

Greg shrugged. "I told you, not much. But after what happened yesterday, I asked around. I talked to one of the twins, and he confirmed that Rob is an odd duck. He's great at his job, but he sucks at people. He usually blurts out things he should keep to himself without even thinking about it, which Jolyn found funny. I'm pretty sure Rob was just shocked about the fact that he's your mate and didn't handle it well."

Payne wanted to believe that. He wanted all of it to have been a misunderstanding and for Rob to give him a chance.

But he was afraid to hope. What if he did, and Rob had been rejecting him, after all? What if he tried talking to Rob, only to be told that he didn't have time to waste on Payne?

Payne wouldn't blame him. He was here to do his job, and he was good at that job. It wouldn't be nice for Payne to distract him, and that was what he was.

A distraction.

He swallowed. "I guess I'll focus on training, and Rob can focus on his job."

Greg glared. "Have you been listening to what I was saying? Because that's not what I told you to do."

"You said I needed to talk to him, and while I believe you're right, I don't think I will."

"Why not?"

"Because he's here to help Jasper. I don't want to distract him."

Greg snorted. "And you don't think that knowing he has a mate in the same house, walking around, isn't going to distract him? I don't care who the guy is. That would be distracting for anyone. If you don't go to him, he'll come to you eventually."

Greg probably wasn't wrong. Just like Payne had a hard time focusing on anything that wasn't Rob, Rob was probably going through the same. It might be a bit different for him because he was human and busy, but eventually, the bond would pull them together. If there was only one reason for them to talk, it was that. They wouldn't be able to ignore the bond between them forever, not even Rob.

But where was Payne supposed to start? What was he supposed to tell Rob? He didn't want to send Rob running, but he also didn't want to be rejected again. He wasn't sure he could stand it, even though he knew it would be for the best, at least when it came to Rob.

What would Rob do with someone like him? It wasn't that Payne wasn't good enough. It was that they were so different that he didn't see a way for them to work together, even though they were mates.

Rob stared at the screen in front of him, but he wasn't seeing it. It was the first time in his life that he couldn't make sense of what he was seeing, and he had no idea what to do about it. He knew what he was *supposed* to do. He was here to help Jasper, go through the documents and data that had been gathered on him, and make his life easier.

Instead, he was daydreaming about Payne and the future they could have together.

It was ridiculous. Rob was thirty-eight, for fuck's sake. He wasn't a lovestruck teenager, and he needed to stop acting like one, especially when he and Payne had barely talked. He hadn't seen Payne since the man had run out of the kitchen without looking back, and he was surprised to realize that he wanted to.

Why? Was it because of the bond? That couldn't be possible, because Rob still believed that was a mistake. Rocco had insisted that a shifter couldn't make mistakes when it came to their mate, but Rob wasn't so sure about that. It was clear he and Payne didn't belong together.

But if that was so, why couldn't he stop thinking about the other man? Why had he dreamed about him last night? Why did he think of him every time his mind wandered?

It had to be because after what happened yesterday, Rob believed Payne was his mate. Logically, he could see how impossible that was, but his heart believed otherwise.

Payne was young and gorgeous. Anyone would be honored to have him in their life, and that went for Rob, too. He hadn't had many lovers because he'd always been so busy with his job, but Payne made him want to dump everything and focus only on him. Rob would be more than happy to take him out to dinner, go on dates, and have a life together.

He shook his head and scowled at the screen. He needed to stop obsessing over this, dammit. He wasn't doing his job, which was the reason he was here. If he couldn't do his job, what good was he for?

"You're driving me nuts," Rocco said, his voice almost a

growl.

Rob looked away from his screen, blinking. Rocco was sitting in the corner of the infirmary, working on his own files. As a doctor, especially one who dealt with a secret group of genetically modified assassins who couldn't go to a normal hospital, he was always learning and looking into new procedures. That was what he was supposed to be doing, but clearly, Rob had been distracting him.

Rob rubbed his eyes. "I apologize. Maybe I should take my computer and head up to my room. That way I won't bother you."

Rocco turned his chair around to face Rob. "Or maybe you could do something about the reason why you're distracted."

"I don't know what you're talking about."

"You know what I'm talking about, so stop bullshitting me. Tell me what the problem is with Payne."

Rob shook his head, but at the same time, he twisted to face Rocco and started talking. "I just don't understand it, and I feel guilty. I'm still not a hundred percent sure that Payne hasn't made a mistake, but what am I going to do if he hasn't?"

Rocco cocked his head. "Well, you know what mates usually do."

Rob waved his words away. "Yes, I know they get together and bond and are happy for the rest of their lives. How is that fair to Payne, though?"

"You lost me."

"Look at me and look at him. What I said yesterday still stands. We don't fit together, and it's not fair to him to be saddled with an old man who knows computers and science better than people."

"First of all, you're not an old man."

"I realize you don't feel that way because you're a shifter, but I'm very much human, and I'm thirty-eight. I'm not middle-aged yet, but I will be sooner rather than later, while Payne is only twenty." And he looked his age. "He should have better than a grumpy old man who gets lost in his work and forgets to eat, let alone that he has friends."

If Rob was honest, Rocco was his only friend. He'd lost everyone else over the years, and maybe he should feel sorry about that, but he didn't. He'd never been one to have many friends, or friends at all, really. Even when he was younger, he never felt like he needed anyone in his life. Maybe that made him strange, and maybe it was sad, but it was what it was. He didn't miss having friends.

So why did he feel like he needed Payne?

"You realize that Payne feels the same, right?"

Rob frowned. "What are you talking about?"

"If you think you're too old for him and that it would be better if he were with someone his age and who shares his interests, what do you believe he's thinking? He's twenty, has just started living his life after going through hell, and only now discovering what he can do with it. Yet, here you are, older, doing important work, and knowing what you want with your life. How can he not feel intimidated by that?"

"You're right," a voice said from the open door.

Both Rob and Rocco turned to face it. Payne stood there, looking extremely nervous. He shuffled his feet and carefully didn't look at Rob, but Rob couldn't look away from him.

Payne really was gorgeous. He was the most beautiful man Rob had ever seen, although maybe that had to do with the fact that Rob didn't usually pay attention to people. What did it matter if they were beautiful? What was more important was the way they thought and what was inside their mind.

But Payne was beautiful. His blond hair was short, and his body was the body of a fighter. Rob knew that Payne had been training with the assassins, so it made sense. Rob remembered from yesterday that Payne's eyes were brown, a deep, warm color that made him want to lose himself in them. Payne was slender, yet he looked much stronger than Rob.

Not that Rob cared about that. He wasn't a fighter, and he didn't keep himself in shape, even though he was very much aware of the fact that he should. He always had too much work to do, and skipping meals, albeit unintentionally, meant he stayed slim. That wouldn't last forever, especially since he was nearing forty, but it was good enough for now. He'd make changes when the time came.

Maybe the time *had* come.

"Payne," Rocco said with a smile. "What can I do for you? Or are you here to talk to Rob?"

Payne looked at Rob.

His cheeks were flushed, and it added to his appeal. He was very clearly an adult, but the flush was endearing and made Rob want to protect him and offer him the moon.

"I'd like to talk to Rob if it's possible. I don't want to bother you, though, so I can wait."

Rob blinked. "Why would you wait?" He shouldn't have to. If he truly was Rob's mate, he was supposed to be the center of Rob's life.

Payne shrugged. "You're working. I know how important it is, and I don't want to be a bother."

Rob shot to his feet, startling himself, Rocco, and Payne, who stepped back into the hallway.

"You're not a bother," Rob said, perhaps too firmly.

Payne looked startled. "All right. Can you talk now, then?"

"Yes." Rob looked back at his computer and grimaced. "Give me a moment to save the work I was doing, and I'll be right with you."

"Sure. I'll be out here, waiting." He turned and disappeared into the hallway.

Rob looked at Rocco, already panicking. "What am I supposed to do? What do I tell him?"

Rocco's smile was gentle. "Be honest with him. It's the only thing you can do and what both of you deserve."

Honest. Rob could do that.

Or at least, he hoped so.

Payne wished he were anywhere but here. He didn't want to do this. He didn't want to ask Rob what he thought about them being mates or what his plans were. He was terrified of what Rob would tell him.

But he'd been through so much worse than being rejected by his mate. Even if Rob didn't want him, he'd survive. It would be hard for a while, but he didn't need his mate in his life. He wanted him, but he could deal without him, too.

It was that knowledge that had pushed Payne to look for Rob. He'd known he'd find the man in the infirmary because that was where he'd been since he'd arrived. And now, they were about to talk, and Payne was scared.

Shouldn't meeting your mate feel good? He'd always believed that was the case, although considering the situations in which the people he lived with had been over the years, maybe he shouldn't have. Most of their meetings with their mates had been complicated, yet they'd managed to work things out in the end.

Would Payne and Rob be able to do so? Or was their relationship doomed from the beginning?

"Are we going to talk here?"

"Not if you don't want everyone in the building to know what we're saying."

Rob blinked.

He shouldn't be adorable at his age, but he was. He reminded Payne of a confused owl, with his glasses and the way he cocked his head to the side.

"I would rather not," Rob said.

That was what Payne had expected. "They're only a few spots I can think of that can be private enough for us to have a chat that will stay between us."

"You choose. You know the house better than I do."

Payne's bedroom was out, so the roof it was.

Payne led the way down the hallway, both eager and dreading getting to the roof. The roof was wide, and it was divided into several smaller spaces to give anyone space to be alone if they wished for it. It was where a lot of the assassins and their mates had their dates, and sometimes Payne had walked in on them in positions in which he wished he hadn't seen them. Everyone in the warehouse was an adult, though, so no harm no foul, but Payne keenly felt his lack of experience when it came to sex.

Maybe that was one of the reasons Rob didn't want anything to do with him. Maybe somehow he knew Payne had never been with anyone, and he didn't want to have to deal with that.

And maybe Payne was freaking out for nothing. He seriously needed to stop and take whatever would happen next when it came.

"What's on the roof?" Rob asked as they walked.

"You haven't been yet?"

"I haven't had a reason to. I've been spending most of my time in the infirmary."

"Well, the roof is a communal area. There are couches, a dining area with a grill, and several areas that have been made more private. In a house with so many people, it's not always easy to have your own space, and while it's not like our private bedrooms, it's a place where we can go when we need time and peace."

"And no one will be there to listen to us?"

"A few people might be, but I'm sure we'll find a private spot to talk."

Rob nodded, apparently satisfied. He seemed to trust Payne, but Payne wasn't sure what to make of any of this. "What does Rob stand for?" he asked after a moment. He didn't like silence, especially not with his mate. He felt the need to fill it, which was probably ridiculous, but he couldn't stop himself.

"I'm just a boring Robert," Rob said.

"You're not boring."

"Trust me. Once you get to know me, you'll realize that I very much am."

Payne could have sworn that wouldn't be the case, but something told him Rob wouldn't believe him. He'd thought Rob had rejected him because Payne wasn't good enough for him, but maybe not. Maybe a part of Rob was insecure about himself, even though Payne couldn't imagine it.

He was relieved when they got to the roof. It was softly raining, not enough to stop him and Rob from having their chat, but enough that everyone else was downstairs or out. He led the way toward his favorite spot in a corner of the roof.

It had been closed off on three sides by light wooden walls, and it was covered. They had to run to get there without getting too wet, but that was fine. It made Rob smile, and he was even more handsome when he smiled.

Two couches and a small table had been placed under the gazebo. Payne flopped on one of them while Rob sat on the edge of the other as if he expected to have to run. Payne disliked the thought of his mate being nervous when he was with him, but he was very much nervous when he was with Rob, so he could understand the feeling.

"What about you? Payne is an interesting name," Rob said.

He couldn't know the story behind Payne's name, and while Payne hesitated to tell him, he decided to do so in the end. If he and Rob wanted a chance to be together, Rob would eventually find out about Payne's past. That wasn't why they were here, but it also wasn't something Payne wanted to avoid talking about.

"The woman who bought me called me that. She always said I was a pain in the ass."

Rob frowned. "I'm afraid I don't understand."

"This isn't what I wanted to tell you, but I suppose you should know. I don't remember my parents. To be honest, I don't know where I was born or how old I am exactly. The first thing I remember is a woman. She was human, and she bought me at an auction. She forced me to stay in my fennec fox form most of the time, and I don't remember if I had a name before her. Beck has been trying to find out more about my past, but he hasn't been able to find anything, and at this point, I'm not sure it matters anymore."

Rob looked horrified. "An auction?"

Payne nodded curtly. "It happens. Humans, but also supernatural creatures, buy children at auctions. They especially like cute shifters, and they keep us in our shifter form like pets. Then they sell us back once we're older and buy younger kids."

Rob swallowed loudly. "How did you end up with the assassins?"

"They saved us. They killed the man who auctioned us, and they took us away. Most of the kids were younger, but Greg and I were old enough to understand what was happening. We didn't have a home to go back to, and we asked if we could stay here with the assassins. They agreed, and we've been here for four years now."

"I'm sorry all of that happened to you."

"It's in the past. I guess I wanted you to know because this way, you can see that even though I'm much younger than you, it doesn't mean my life has been easy."

"I never thought it had been."

"I know what hardship is. None of that changes the fact

that we're mates."

Rob pressed his lips together, but he didn't say anything. Payne waited, but when Rob still didn't continue, he felt the need to speak again.

"I realize how different we are and that maybe it isn't appealing to you, and if that's the case, I'll understand. There's nothing I can do to change my age, and neither can you. But I *can* promise you that I know what I want with my life, even though I'm young. I'm going to be a council assassin, and I'm going to help people like they helped Greg and me. I've already been accepted into a program, so you don't have to worry about having to babysit me or anything like that. I just want you to give us a chance. You don't have to make promises, and we don't have to bond anytime soon. Just, please, give us a chance."

Payne had already lost so much in his life, and he didn't want to lose his mate, too. But the only one who could decide what would happen next between them was Rob, and he wasn't talking.

Rob could hear Payne's voice becoming more panicky, and that was the last thing he wanted.

He raised a hand, and Payne pressed his lips together. He looked like he wanted to continue rambling, but Rob was afraid he'd say something he'd regret. He'd already said so much, telling Rob about his past.

Rob was horrified. His life wasn't exciting, but it was good. He'd grown up with two loving parents, and while unfortunately he'd lost both of them—albeit in different ways—because they'd been elderly when he'd been born, he'd had a great childhood. He'd never wanted for anything, and he still didn't. His parents had supported him through college, and they'd always been there for him up until his father died and his mother got dementia.

But Payne hadn't known anything like that. From what he'd said, he hadn't known anything but pain, including his name. The last thing Rob wanted was to hurt Payne even more. Payne needed to understand how he was, though. Otherwise, they could never work as a couple.

And yes, Rob was seriously considering dating Payne.

"I apologize," he said stiffly. "I don't want you to panic, but this is how I face big decisions. I take time to think about it."

Payne blinked. "You're telling me this as if you expect me to get used to it."

"I suppose I do. If we're going to be together, I don't want you to freak out every time I close myself off. I realize I'm going to have to change that behavior, but knowing myself, it won't be easy. It'll take me some time to open up to you."

"I'm confused. Yesterday, you said it was impossible that we were mates. Now, you're behaving as if the fact that we'll be together is a given."

Rob rubbed his face. "See? This is what I meant yesterday. I have no idea how to do any of this. I'm not romantic, and I don't do relationships. You deserve so much better, so much *more*, but unfortunately, you're stuck with me."

Payne stared for a moment, his mouth slightly open in what might be surprise. "Wait," he said eventually. "When you said it wasn't possible, it was because you think I should have someone better?"

At least he seemed to understand. "Exactly. Look at us. You're incredibly gorgeous, just starting your life, and you have the entire world waiting for you. Why would you want to be held back by me? I'm much older, grumpy on the best of days, and entirely too focused on my work. If we were together, I'd probably neglect you, and you'd get angry, and we'd fight, and eventually, we'd break up."

"You can't know that."

"Not for sure, but I know myself. I'm very much aware of how complicated life with me can be. I've had a few relationships before, but all of them have fizzled out, and it was entirely my fault."

"You can't be sure of that."

The fact that Payne wanted to defend him made Rob smile. "I very much can be. As I just explained, I don't know how to be in a relationship or how to make sure you get the attention you deserve. I lose myself in my work. Sometimes I go more than a day without eating because I forget I have to. If I can't even take care of myself, how can I take care of you?"

Payne leaned forward. "So what you're saying is that I deserve better."

Even though it hurt to admit it, Rob nodded. He wasn't sure when he'd gone from denying that he and Payne could be together to not wanting to lose Payne, but that was how he felt. Damn mate bond. "So much better," he said. "You deserve someone who will be there for you whenever you need him. You deserve someone who will look at you the way I look at my work."

"And you don't think you can give me that?"

"I'm not sure I can. As I said, I've never been in a committed relationship, not for long. There's a good reason for that, and I don't want to hurt you, something I'm sure I will do."

Payne leaned back, crossing his arms over his chest. "I'm sorry, but that's bullshit."

Rob blinked. "What?"

"I understand where you're coming from, and I'm sure all of this can become a problem eventually if we don't face it. But you don't get to tell me what I deserve. I'm the only one who can make that decision."

"I agree. You have to see that I can't be the man you need me to be, though."

Payne shook his head. "I don't. You're my mate, and there's a reason for that. You wouldn't be my mate if we weren't meant to be together."

Rob had been afraid of that. The bond was influencing Payne, which meant he couldn't be objective about this. Rob couldn't say he was sorry. He didn't want to lose Payne, even though they weren't even together yet.

And when had he decided that he and Payne should be together?

He doubted Payne would admit the truth that was right in front of him when he didn't know Rob. There was only one way for him to be aware of what he was getting into, and it was to spend time with him. Rob was terrified that by the end of it, Payne would see the truth and dump him, but he couldn't help but wonder what would happen if he didn't.

Could they be together? Could they be happy as a couple? There was only one way for them to find out.

"I suggest we get to know each other," he said slowly. "It's the only way we can decide whether or not we should be together."

Payne's expression turned stubborn. "We should. We wouldn't be mates if we weren't supposed to be together."

"I'm sure you're right, but I have a bit more difficulty accepting this. To be honest, I never expected to be anyone's mate. I can barely be someone's boyfriend, and that never ends well. I still believe that eventually you'll realize how much better you would be without me and that you'll leave."

"I'm not going to. I might only be twenty, but I would never do something that stupid."

"I believe that you believe you won't. That's why I suggested we get to know each other. That way, you'll get to find out how aggravating I am. I guarantee you that you'll want to run away screaming after a few days."

Payne leaned forward again, but he didn't limit himself to

that this time. He also grabbed one of Rob's hands and squeezed it before linking their fingers together.

Rob couldn't look away. When was the last time anyone had held his hand? It had probably been his mother the last time he'd visited, and the memory made his chest feel tight.

"And I can guarantee you that I'm not going anywhere," Payne promised. He raised Rob's hand and kissed the back of it. He looked flustered as he did so, but that didn't stop him. "But fine. We'll do things your way. Maybe once this is done, you'll see that we do belong together, no matter how awful you think you are."

Payne got to his feet. Rob panicked at the thought of him leaving, but Payne smiled at him. "I'm going to go get something to eat. Do you need anything?"

"No, thank you."

"Then I'll see you later. Sit next to me when you come to dinner, all right?"

Rob could only nod and watch Payne walk away. He'd come into this meeting convinced that he and Payne would both agree they were better off being on their own. Instead, Payne had somehow convinced Rob to give their relationship a try.

How had *that* happened?

CHAPTER THREE

Payne was so nervous that he felt like he might be about to jump out of his skin. He was tempted to stop obsessing over what was about to happen and think of Rob instead, but he wasn't sure it would be better or worse.

He had no idea where he and Rob stood. He thought he'd managed to convince Rob to give them a chance, but things were still weird between them. Rob seemed bewildered, as if he didn't understand why Payne wanted to be with him. Maybe he truly didn't. Payne had been stunned when Rob admitted he thought he wasn't good enough for him, and he didn't know how to make Rob see that wasn't the case.

Would things work between them if they both believed the other deserved better? Payne wasn't sure, but he supposed they'd find out. As long as they both gave their relationship a chance, he believed things would be okay.

"Ready?" Dasha asked.

Payne and Greg looked at each other. Payne grimaced, but he still nodded and took one of Dasha's hands. Greg did the same, but before shimmering them away, Dasha looked from one to the other. "You do realize you don't have to do this if you don't want to, right?"

By now, everyone in the warehouse knew that Greg and Payne had been offered a spot in the program and that they'd accepted it. It was impossible for anyone to have secrets here, but Payne and Greg hadn't tried hiding it. They were proud of it, and Payne was still convinced it was the right thing to do.

But he was also nervous.

"We want this," Greg said.

Dasha smiled. "But you're nervous."

"Wouldn't you be? Were you nervous when you were recruited to become an assassin?" Because even though Dasha was a Nix, he didn't have any special ability. Mostly, he'd been pulled onto the team to shimmer the assassins back and forth, although he did participate in some missions when he had to.

"Honestly?" Dasha asked. He looked around as if he expected someone to listen to their conversation, but the shimmering room was empty except for them. "I'm still nervous most of the time."

Greg chuckled, but Payne's stomach churned. If Dasha, who'd been an assassin for years, was still nervous, how could he ever stop feeling that way?

Dasha continued, "I'm sure you'll be okay. You're not going on a mission. Today, you're just going to meet the people you'll be training with and your trainers. This is what the two of you have wanted for a long time, right?"

Greg and Payne nodded as one. "We have," Greg confirmed.

"Then you'll be fine. You'll learn how to work together and with others and how to be assassins. You won't go out on missions right away, and even if you feel like you suck, remember that you're not assassins yet."

"You talk as if you already know we're going to suck," Payne pointed out.

Dasha chuckled. "I don't, but I remember my training. Nervousness is good, Payne. It means you'll be careful."

With that, he shimmered them out of the room. Greg had been holding Dasha's other hand, and Payne turned to look at him as soon as they arrived wherever they were going. Win had given them the address and told them a bit about it, but

Payne didn't know what to expect.

He dropped Dasha's hand and looked around. They'd shimmered into a room created for that purpose. The only thing he could see around him were cement walls and floor. There was a door in one of the walls, and it was open.

He and Greg looked at each other again. That was where they were supposed to go, wasn't it?

"I can stay for a bit if you want me to," Dasha offered.

Payne shook his head. "We'll be fine."

"All right. Let me know when it's time for you to go home, and I'll pick you up."

"Thank you."

"Don't worry. It'll be great."

With that, Dasha was gone, and Greg and Payne were alone.

Payne stared at the open door for a second. If he and Greg were going to do this, they needed to do it. Yes, they were nervous, but they knew what they were signing up for. They might as well start. Besides, it wouldn't be good to arrive late on their first day.

"What do you think we'll do today?" he asked Greg as they walked down the hallway. Everything was cement here, too, but they could see another door at the end of the hallway. There was a tiny window in it, and sunshine streamed through it.

"We'll probably be introduced to the other trainees and trainers. Maybe they'll ask us to fight for a bit, just to see our level."

Something settled in Payne's chest. That, he could do. He'd been training with the assassins for the past four years. He knew he was good at fighting hand-to-hand, and he had some experience with weapons.

He could do this. They both could.

Greg pushed open the second door, and they stepped out

of the building. Payne blinked and looked around, curious.

The first thing he noticed was that the space where they stood was surrounded by trees. They seemed to be in an enormous clearing in the middle of a forest or something similar. The air was cool but not cold, and the sun shone.

The building behind them was small, but there were more, and those were bigger. Even from where he was, he could see that each of the buildings sported a different letter painted on its side, which made sense when he saw the indications panel just in front of the building from which they'd come out.

He took a step closer and peered at it. "Where are we supposed to meet the others?"

"In front of building C," Greg answered. "Win said that's where most of the training happens."

It was on the panel. Each letter was labeled, so Payne knew that building C held the classrooms and gyms, building A was administrative, building B held the equipment, and building D was where the trainees and the trainers lived. Apparently, it included a cafeteria.

The shimmering building in which they'd arrived was set aside from the others and labeled building E.

"Well, it's this way," he told Greg.

Greg nodded and checked the watch on his wrist. They'd agreed to arrive early, just in case something went wrong, and Payne was glad. It gave both of them a moment to breathe, wrap their minds around what was about to happen, and hopefully, calm down. He didn't want to be a nervous mess by the time he met the others.

"Have you talked to Evan?" he asked Greg as they walked.

"About this, you mean?"

"Yeah."

Greg shrugged. "He's fine with it. He knows I'm nervous, but he pretty much gave me the same speech as Dasha. He also pointed out that the others probably aren't as well trained as we are."

"Well, they haven't trained with the assassins for years."

"Exactly. He mentioned listening to the trainers if what they say contradicts what we know, but I guess we'll see."

Payne nodded. He and Greg didn't have to be perfect. They just had to be here and try, and everything would be fine.

They found building C easily, thanks to the massive letter painted on it. Payne would have known that was where they were going even without the letter, though. A small group of people had gathered in front of the building, and he suspected they were the new trainees he and Greg would be working with.

His stomach churned again.

By the time they reached the group, everyone was looking at them. Payne didn't blame them, because he was staring back. The future council assassins were a mismatched group of men and women, most of them young, but some in their thirties, from what Payne could guess. He wondered if all of them had a special ability and if he and Greg would find that maybe they weren't good enough next to those people. He kind of resented them for having abilities, while at the same time, he was glad he didn't have one. He was very much aware of how special abilities were forced on shifters, other supernatural creatures, and even humans. He'd already been through enough in his life without wanting to spend time in a lab, too.

"Hey," someone said.

Payne looked from Greg to the man who'd spoken. He was a Nix, so he had green eyes, pointed ears, and blond hair. His hair was cut short, making his ears look even more pointed.

"Hey," Payne answered.

"My name is Seymour."

"I'm Payne, and this is Greg."

Seymour nodded. "Pleasure to meet you, I guess."

Greg snorted. "You don't have to sound so enthusiastic."

Thankfully, instead of getting offended, Seymour grinned. "I'm feeling a bit awkward. Aren't you? I mean, I'm never the greatest when I meet new people, but this time is even worse."

Payne felt himself relax. He wasn't the only nervous one.

He could do this. He *was* doing it.

Rob was doing his best to focus on his computer and work, but he couldn't stop thinking about Payne. That seemed to be a regular occurrence these past few days, and he wasn't sure what to do about it or if there was anything he *could* do about it.

Right now, he was wondering how Payne was doing. Payne had been extremely nervous about going to the camp and meeting the people he'd be training with. Several of the assassins had tried to reassure him, and even Rob had, but it had been awkward, to say the least. Rob barely knew Payne, and while he was sure his mate knew what he was doing, he wouldn't have been able to fight his way out of a wet paper bag.

He huffed and leaned back in his chair. Somewhere along the way, he'd started thinking of Payne as his mate, even though he was human and normally humans didn't have mates. Sure, he was Payne's mate, but the other way around didn't work, or at least, that was what he'd thought for a long time. Now, he couldn't help but wonder.

He'd known humans felt the bond, too, but he hadn't realized he'd feel it so strongly. When Payne entered a room, Rob looked up, even if he hadn't heard him or noticed it was him. When he walked into a room, he could tell if Payne was there or not.

Was that normal? It made him feel weird, especially since

as a human, he'd never felt that way. Should he be able to track Payne the way he was?

And how much worse would things be if they bonded?

Rob knew that if he and Payne were bonded, they'd be able to feel each other's emotions. He hadn't needed to be bonded to Payne to know he was nervous this morning, but now, he paused and tried to think about how things would have been if the bond was complete. Would he be able to feel Payne's nervousness even now that Payne was away?

"You look like you're thinking hard," someone said from the infirmary door.

Rob turned to face Jasper. He was smiling, which was a common occurrence these days. In the beginning, Rob hadn't understood how Jasper could be so happy, but he'd come to realize it was thanks to Jasper's mate. Even with everything that had happened to Jasper and everything that continued happening in his life, as long as he was with Frazer, he was happy. He knew Frazer loved him for who he was, not for what he could do or for the way he looked. He knew that Frazer would always be there for him, whatever happened.

Rob had a hard time wrapping his mind around the fact that the same could be said for him and Payne.

Jasper stepped into the infirmary. "You haven't poked at me in a few days. I was getting worried."

Rob gestured at his computer. "I've been going over the data again."

"Anything I can help you with?"

"Not at the moment."

Jasper's smile widened. "I didn't mean just work related. Want to talk about you and Payne?"

Rob groaned. Of course everyone in this place knew about him and Payne. Even if Payne hadn't blurted out that they were mates in front of half a dozen people, Rob had seen how fast news could travel here in the warehouse. He supposed it made sense. With so many people sharing a living space and acting as a family, they all wanted to know what was going on and to help if they could.

Jasper chuckled, grabbed Rocco's chair from the other side of the infirmary, and wheeled closer. He stopped it next to Rob, then flopped into it and continued staring at Rob.

Considering everything, Jasper was doing incredibly well. Physically, he was as fine as he ever would be. He was healthy, and he was learning to deal with the changes that had been done to his body. Sometimes he still had trouble with his heightened strength and speed, and it wasn't unheard of for him to break things without meaning to, but it happened less and less often. The thick crocodile-like skin was still odd to look at and even odder to touch, but it didn't seem to bother Jasper.

"He'll be fine," Jasper said.

Rob didn't have to ask to know who he was talking about. "I know. I never thought he wouldn't be."

Jasper stared at Rob. "Want to tell me what's going on in that super brain of yours?"

Rob didn't, but at the same time, he did. He had no idea what he was doing, and while Jasper was one of his patients, he was also a friend. The lines between work and friendship had blurred since he'd arrived at the warehouse, and he didn't think they'd ever go back to what they'd been before. He didn't want them to, either.

Rob had always been a loner, and he'd never had a problem with that. He still didn't, yet at the same time, he felt as if he'd found a home and family. It was probably stupid, but he wanted to belong here, with these people, and maybe, with him being Payne's mate, he did.

"I'm just not sure how to do any of this," he confessed.

"None of us were sure in the beginning.

"But you have everything under control."

"It might look like it, but I wouldn't be so sure. A lot of it is thanks to Frazer and everyone else. Without them, I'd be entirely lost."

That was probably true. "Well, I'm not. I know what Payne wants and what he deserves, but I don't know if I can give that to him."

"I don't think you'll know until you give yourself a chance to do that. Have you stopped pushing him away?"

"How can I continue to resist? I feel guilty because he's stuck with someone like me, yet at the same time, I'd feel guilty rejecting him, too. Whether I like it or not, I'm his mate. He won't get another one, and I don't want to take this away from him."

Rob was almost grateful when his phone rang, interrupting them. His stomach dropped when he saw the name flashing on the screen. When they called, it was never for a good reason.

He raised a finger to tell Jasper he needed to take this, then he answered. "Rob Pearson."

"I'm sorry to bother you," the nurse said.

"Don't worry about it. Just tell me what happened."

"Nothing bad yet, but she's very agitated today. We've tried everything without success. I thought that maybe if you came, she'd calm down a bit? She'd been talking about your father."

And since Rob's mother didn't recognize him but sometimes thought he was his father, there might be a chance that he could help calm her down. "I'll be there as soon as I can."

"Thank you."

He hung up, already getting to his feet. Jasper looked worried, and he followed Rob, walking with him to the hallway. "Can I ask what happened?"

"It's my mother. She has dementia, and she's in a home, but they just called me. She's agitated."

"I'm sorry. Why don't you find one of the twins? They can shimmer you to her. That way, you don't have to find a way around the secrecy of this place."

Rob swore. He'd almost opened the app to get a Nix to come to pick him up. Maybe he should cancel the app, since he couldn't use it while he lived in the warehouse. "I don't want to bother them."

"You won't. There's no one in the infirmary, which means the twins aren't working. They'll be more than happy to help you get to your mother."

Rob hoped so, because he needed to get there as soon as he could. She'd never hurt herself when she was agitated, but he didn't want her to start today.

His heart broke a little every time he saw her. It was an odd sensation, even though he knew what was happening. Externally, she was still his mother, but her mind wasn't there anymore. She hadn't been able to recognize him in months, and he felt he'd lost the last piece of his mother. But her body was still here, and he was still taking care of it, plus whatever was left of her in it. He'd made a promise to his father before he'd died, and Rob had every intention of keeping that promise, no matter how much it hurt.

And it did. But maybe it was a pain Rob didn't have to shoulder on his own anymore. That was an odd sensation, too, and he wasn't sure he wanted to tell Payne about his mother, but he knew that if he needed to talk or anything else, Payne would be there for him.

"Good job today," Jamison said, clapping his hands.

Payne was breathing hard. He looked down at Kerwin, who was flat on his back in the grass. Payne had been the one to put him there, but Kerwin didn't seem offended. Instead, he grinned widely, then reached up for Payne's hand.

Payne was careful as he took Kerwin's, just in case Kerwin tried to pull him down, but he didn't. Payne helped the demon to his feet, then they both turned toward Jamison, their trainer.

"That's enough for today," Jamison said. "Go to your dorm rooms, shower, and find your way around. You'll be here a while, and I want you to be comfortable and feel like this is your home."

Payne caught Greg's gaze. He was on the other side of the stretch of grass, working with Seymour. He and Payne wouldn't be living here, and while that was a relief, it also made things awkward.

"You kicked my ass," Kerwin said. His tail lazily swung behind him.

"You weren't that bad."

"Maybe not, but you were better. Where did you learn to fight like that?"

Win had cautioned Greg and Payne about what they said to the others. For now, they barely knew them, and while Payne liked Kerwin and Seymour, and most of the others, he didn't know if he could trust them. They'd eventually become council assassins if they managed to finish training, but for now they were just a bunch of people stuck together.

"My family knows how to fight," he said instead of revealing the truth. It was kind of the truth, anyway.

"Yeah? You're lucky. My mother fainted when I told her I was going to be part of this program." Kerwin grabbed his bottle of water from the edge of the grassy expanse. "She tried to convince me not to come up until this morning."

"But since you're here, she failed."

"Clearly. She wants to protect me, but she doesn't understand that I'm not a child anymore."

"As long as this is what you want, she should respect it."

Unfortunately, Kerwin's grimace told Payne there was a fat

chance of that.

"What do you say, dinner together?" Kerwin asked.

Payne rubbed the back of his neck. "Actually, Greg and I have to head home."

Kerwin blinked. "You're not staying with us here?"

They were the only two who weren't, but Win had thought of a good reason for that. "We're not. We live with our mates."

Kerwin's eyes widened. "You've already met your mate? You're so young."

"So?"

"Nothing. I guess I was just surprised."

Like humans, demons didn't have mates, so Kerwin would never find his, although he might still be a shifter's mate. Payne wasn't sure what to do with Rob, but he was glad he'd met him. "No more surprised than I was. Greg's been with Evan for a few years now, but I just met mine."

"Sometimes, I think you shifters go too fast. You already live with him?"

"There's no reason for me not to, right?"

"I suppose not. I didn't know they were making exceptions about the trainees staying here, though. Are you and Greg the only mated ones?"

"No idea. I'm sure you'll find out tonight, though." Kerwin had a way of making people comfortable, and Payne had no doubt that he'd know everything about everyone by the end of the week.

Kerwin grinned. "Probably. Well, say hello to your mate for me."

The others had started packing up their things. Small groups had formed during the day, as was bound to happen. They were all trainees and in the same position here, but it made sense that they'd become close to some of them. Kerwin felt like a friend already, and Payne kind of liked it.

"Ready to go?" Greg asked as he reached Payne.

"Whenever you're ready."

Greg nodded. "I texted Dasha. He'll be waiting for us in the shimmering room."

They headed that way, leaving the others behind. Payne heard Seymour ask about them and where they were going, and Kerwin answering. He was glad he'd thought of telling Kerwin that he and Greg were both mated, even though he wasn't. He hadn't lied, anyway. He and Rob did live together. They both lived with a whole other bunch of people, though.

"How do you think it went?" Greg asked as they reached building E.

"Pretty well, or at least, I hope so. Jamison and the other trainers didn't have anything to say."

"I saw you kick Kerwin's ass."

"Yeah. He tries to use his tail when he fights, but he's not very good at it."

"Well, I'm sure he'll learn."

That was what they were here for, after all.

As promised, Dasha was already in the shimmering room when Payne and Greg walked in, so it only took them a few seconds to return.

Payne was glad once he got back to the warehouse. He stretched and got a nose full of how badly he smelled. He wrinkled his nose, wondering whether he should shower or eat first, but since he didn't want to kill anyone, he opted for the shower.

He felt better by the time he was clean and wearing comfortable clothes. He and Greg made their way back downstairs, and to Payne's surprise, Rob was standing in the hallway by the stairs.

"Hey," he said, his heart racing. Was Rob waiting for him?

Rob smiled, but his expression told Payne something had happened. Had Rob decided it would be better if he and

Payne weren't together? Was he about to break up with Payne?

"I'll go to the kitchen," Greg said. "Evan's waiting for me."

"I'll be right there," Payne told him.

He waited until Greg was gone to turn back to Rob. "What happened?" he asked, even though it was the last thing he wanted to find out. If Rob was going to dump him, he wanted to know it as soon as possible. It was going to hurt either way.

"Nothing," Rob tried to reassure him.

"That's bullshit. Come on. Tell me what's going on." Payne hesitated. "Did I do something I shouldn't have?"

Rob's eyes widened, and he stepped toward Payne. "Of course not. You've been nothing but perfect since we decided to give this a go."

"If it's not me, what is it?"

Rob sighed. "I don't want to burden you, especially not today of all days."

"I wouldn't be asking you what's going on if I didn't want to know. I don't care what it is. If we're going to be together, you have to be able to lean on me, just like I'll want to lean on you if I need it."

Rob stared at him for a moment, then finally nodded. Payne was relieved, because it seemed that Rob was going to tell him what was going on, but he was also anxious. He wanted to help Rob, but he had no idea whether or not he'd be able to.

"I got a phone call from the home where my mother lives today," Rob said.

They hadn't talked about Rob's family yet, so Payne waited.

"She has dementia," Rob continued. "I've been taking care of her since my father passed away a few years ago. She doesn't recognize me most of the time. The nurse called me because she couldn't settle down, but she did settle once I got there. I thought it was my presence, but she called me by my father's name."

"I'm sorry." What else could Payne say? He wished this were an enemy he could fight for Rob, but nothing he or anyone else did would help.

Rob's smile was sad. "It's fine."

"It's not, but I'm still sorry. Do you want to tell me about her? Is there anything I can do to help?"

Rob stared at Payne for a moment as if he couldn't quite believe that Payne was there.

Payne understood because he felt the same way. He didn't know what Rob saw when he looked at him, but he knew what he saw when he looked at Rob. Rob was his future, whether or not they were both able to admit it at the moment. Eventually, it would be easier for them to accept and live with it. No matter how hard it was at the moment, though, Payne had every intention of being there for Rob. Maybe helping him with his mother or whatever else he needed would show Rob that, no matter what they both believed, they *were* perfect for each other.

And if Rob still couldn't believe it, Payne would have to find another way to convince him.

Rob was touched that Payne wanted to help, even though there was nothing he or anyone else could do. If there had been any treatment for his mother's illness, Rob would have already made sure she got it.

"Anyway, I didn't want to talk about my mother," he said.

"Maybe not, but it's clear you *need* to talk about her."

Payne had said he'd be there for Rob if Rob needed him, but Rob hadn't been sure whether or not to believe him. Payne was so young, and Rob still expected him to lose interest eventually. But maybe he wouldn't. Maybe he truly was in

Rob's life to stay.

"It's hard," he said. He took a chance and reached for Payne's hand. Payne was startled, but he allowed Rob to take it and link their fingers together. Then when Rob pulled Payne down the hallway, Payne came without hesitation.

Payne's hand was dry and warm, and it fit perfectly against Rob's. Rob had always found the way people talked about their mates corny and unrealistic, but he was starting to understand that they'd been right, and he'd been wrong.

"I can only imagine," Payne whispered.

"It's like someone took over my mother's body. Sometimes, I still recognize her, but she's a person I've never met most of the time. She doesn't have the memories that make her *her*, you know?"

"I'm not sure how dementia works. I've never had to deal with it."

"Well, the first to go were the most recent memories." Rob had no intention of going into the technical aspects of dementia, but he could explain to Payne why it hurt so much to see his mother like this. "In the beginning, we didn't realize what was happening. Even when I started thinking that it could be that, I didn't want to believe it. I thought it was just that she was getting older. I took her to the doctor, and they told us about the dementia. She's been declining steadily for the past few years, and while she recognized me almost every time I visited until recently, it's getting worse."

Rob had studied dementia when he'd found out his mother had it, so he knew it was different for each person. He'd tried keeping her at home with him for as long as possible, but eventually she'd reached a stage in which he wasn't enough for her anymore. Right now, she needed constant supervision to make sure she didn't hurt herself or others. She also needed help washing up and dressing, and sometimes eating. Her personality was still the same, but the nurses had told Rob that they were starting to see changes there, too.

He didn't know how he'd deal with the next step of the illness.

But he would because he had to. His mother had taken care of him when he was a child, and now it was time for him to take care of her.

"I already told you I've never known my parents, right?" Payne asked.

They were walking slowly, as if neither of them wanted to get to the kitchen. Payne had to be starving after training all day, but Rob was glad they had this moment to talk and be alone.

"I'm sorry you didn't."

Payne shook his head. "I'm over that. I mean, when I was a kid, I dreamed that my father or my mother would find me and take me away, almost like superheroes. It never happened. I'm not sure if they're dead or if I was taken from them and they couldn't find me."

"I'm sure they're still looking for you, if they're alive."

"That's why I asked Beck to look into it. I don't know what I'll do if he finds out that my parents are still living, but it hasn't happened so far. I got over it, anyway. I'm not angry at them or anything. I have no way to know how I was taken from them, and at this point, it doesn't matter anymore. What I was trying to say is that while I might not fully understand what you're going through, I want you to know that if you need anything, you can talk to me."

"Because we're mates?"

"Because of that, and because sometimes, people just need someone to talk to. I'd like to be that someone, but I'll understand if you'd rather talk to Jasper or Rocco."

Rob shook his head. "There's no one I'd rather talk to than you."

The smile Payne gave him made all the awkwardness Rob

felt worth it.

"But I don't want you to pity me," Payne said. "My life wasn't easy, but the assassins found me when I was sixteen, and I've been happy since then. They gave me an opportunity I never thought I'd have, and while Armand isn't my father, he saved me. I guess that's why I see him as a father figure."

Rob wasn't surprised that was the kind of relationship they shared. Armand had been angry on Payne's behalf the day Rob and Payne had found out they were mates. The man clearly cared for Payne, and Rob was glad Payne had someone like that in his life.

They'd stopped walking a bit ago, and now Rob realized they were alone in the hallway. He could hear people gathered in the kitchen, the sound of silverware against the ceramic plates, even the TV, but here in the hallway, it felt as if he and Payne were in their own little world. He never wanted it to end, but he needed to feed Payne after his tiring day.

He pulled Payne toward the kitchen, but Payne pulled back, stopping him.

"What is it?" Rob asked.

Payne leaned closer and quickly kissed Rob on the lips.

It left Rob blinking and wondering what had happened, but Payne's eyes had gone wide.

"I'm sorry. I should have kissed you on the cheek," he rushed to say.

"It's fine."

"It's just that you looked so sad, and I wanted to cheer you up."

Happiness like nothing Rob could remember exploded in his chest. Payne wanted him, didn't he? He didn't care that Rob was older, grumpy on the best of days, and more focused on his work than anything else. He truly wanted to give this a try.

Payne was still babbling about how sorry he was, and Rob

shut him up by kissing him again. Payne made a surprised noise, but his arms instantly wrapped around Rob's neck, and he pressed closer. His lips parted, and Rob pushed in.

He couldn't remember the last time he'd kissed someone. That probably meant it had been too long, so he decided to take things as slow as possible. Besides, they were in the hallway, where anyone could walk in on them at any second. Considering Rob had already walked in on Rocco making out with his mate in the infirmary several times, he wouldn't be surprised if that happened.

He felt one of Payne's hands creep up his neck until Payne could bury his fingers into his hair. He gently pulled, and Rob groaned loudly enough that he was surprised no one came from the kitchen to make sure everything was all right.

They needed to slow down, but for once, Rob didn't want to. He wanted to push ahead and find out how he and Payne would fit together in bed.

Instead, he took a step back, swallowed, and tried to breathe.

Payne stared at him. His eyes were wide and his pupils blown, and he had the look of someone who'd just been well kissed. Rob was incredibly smug that he'd been the one to do that, and he almost didn't recognize himself. He wasn't usually possessive or anything like that, but he never wanted anyone to see Payne in this state other than him.

"You kissed me," Payne said.

"You kissed me first," Rob pointed out.

"But I was convinced you didn't want to kiss me."

"Why wouldn't I want to?"

Payne shrugged. "I guess that even though you said you wanted us to get to know each other, I wasn't sure if it was the truth or if you'd said that just to make me happy."

Rob took Payne's hand again and squeezed. "I'm starting to believe that making you happy will make me happy, too," he murmured.

"Same goes for me."

They stared at each other for a moment. For all that Rob hadn't believed they could work, he was changing his mind. No matter how young Payne was, what he'd gone through meant that he had more life experience than most people, possibly even more than Rob. There was no way to know if things would work between them, but Rob truly wanted to find out.

CHAPTER FOUR

Wallace dropped his tray on the table in front of Payne and flopped onto the bench. He grabbed the bottle of water from the tray, twisted it open, and took a long sip. When he put it down, he sighed in pleasure.

"They really work us hard," he said.

Payne's mouth was full, but he nodded in agreement. Their four trainers, Jamison, Rhonda, Kennedy, and Hawthorne really did work them hard. Payne didn't mind, because it was what he'd wanted for four years, but he could see some of the others were having trouble with it. He was getting to know all of them, and he hoped no one would drop out because it was getting too hard. They should if that was how they felt, but Payne couldn't imagine this program without all of the participants.

It had been several weeks since he and Greg had started training. In the beginning, things had been awkward, with the two of them leaving at the end of every day while the others stayed together. It hadn't made a difference in how friendly everyone was, especially after Kerwin had told them that it was because Greg and Payne were mated. They were still included in everything the others planned, including the tiny party in Kerwin's dorm room that Hawthorne had shut down when he found out about it.

"But you and Greg are doing great," Wallace continued as he grabbed his fork. He poked at the chicken on his plate, almost as if he didn't trust it was good enough to eat.

"All of us are doing great," Payne said.

"I wouldn't say that. I'm honestly thinking about dropping out."

Payne looked at Wallace. The man was staring at his plate, but his cheeks were flushed. It was easy to see, since his skin was so pale. Wallace's entire body was pale, from his blond hair to his light blue eyes. It was almost as if the printer had run out of ink halfway through printing him.

Payne leaned over the table. "Why do you want to drop out? Is this not what you expected?"

Wallace laughed deprecatingly. "It's what I expected."

"Then what's the problem?"

Wallace shrugged. "My older brother is an enforcer. My father was in the human military. The entire family does this kind of job, and they'd always looked down on me for not doing the same."

Payne had no idea how to deal with families. He'd never had one, at least not until he'd moved in with the assassins. The assassins were an odd family, though. They didn't expect much from him, at least not when it came to this kind of thing. Yes, he was supposed to do chores, his homework, and make sure he graduated from high school, but he'd been allowed to choose what he wanted to do with his life, which was becoming a council assassin. The same couldn't be said for Wallace, and Payne wondered why he'd accepted the opportunity.

Payne didn't begrudge Wallace. He had no idea if the council would have invited someone else if he hadn't said yes, but he hoped he wouldn't have to find out. He liked Wallace, although admittedly, he *was* a bit of a disaster when it came to training.

"Do they know you're here?"

"I wasn't allowed to tell them, was I?"

Right, because not everyone lived with council assassins who knew what was going on. "Then if this isn't what you want, maybe you should drop out. I mean, it's not like they'll find out that you did."

Wallace's eyes narrowed. "Why are you telling me to drop out?"

"Because you said you were thinking about it?" Sometimes, Payne didn't understand people. He couldn't help but wonder if that had to do with how he grew up. As a child, he'd been forced to stay in his fox form most of the time, and the only social interaction he'd had was with people who saw him as a pet and nothing more. Maybe he'd be better at understanding people if he hadn't been in that situation.

"Thinking about it doesn't mean I'm going to do it."

Payne was more and more confused, but Wallace was looking at him as if he expected him to insist he should drop out, and Payne wasn't about to do that. Instead, he leaned back and nodded. "Well, I hope you won't."

Wallace blinked. "You do?"

"Of course. I don't want any of us to drop out."

"Yeah, me neither. We've all become friends, haven't we?"

And Payne was happy about that. The assassins were his friends, but they felt more like family. Greg was his best friend, and it was great, but Payne had always wanted more people in his life. He couldn't be entirely honest with the people he trained with, at least not right now, but they filled a need he hadn't realized he had.

Thankfully, the conversation was interrupted when someone flopped on the bench next to Wallace. Wallace and Payne both turned to look at Kerwin, who grinned at them before turning his attention to his plate. "Did I interrupt something?" he asked. "Payne, you better hope your mate won't see you talking like this with Wallace."

Payne rolled his eyes. After he'd found out that both Payne and Greg were mated, Kerwin had started teasing them. Payne didn't have the heart to tell him that Greg's mate could find him and kill him in his sleep, and no one would ever know what happened. On the other hand, Rob could talk about genetics and whatever he was working on and get Kerwin to fall asleep in seconds.

Or at least, that was how Payne sometimes felt when Rob talked about his work.

"He wouldn't care," Payne said with a smile.

Kerwin blinked. "You realize that's the first time you've said anything about your mate to me, right? I didn't even know it was a guy."

Payne had been keeping it to himself for a reason, but now that several weeks had passed, he felt he trusted his new friends. He couldn't tell them about the assassins yet, not without talking to Win first, but he could tell them about Rob. He'd asked Rob a few days ago, and his mate hadn't seen a problem with telling his new friends about him.

That had surprised Payne. He didn't know what had changed between them, but he could tell something had. Maybe it was because Payne had been there for Rob after he'd gone to see his mother, or maybe Rob had given in to the inevitable. Whatever the reason, Payne felt they were working toward a real relationship, and he couldn't have been happier.

"So you and Gregory are really mated?" Wallace asked.

Payne wished Greg were here, but he'd stayed back to talk to Rhonda and Kennedy when training had ended. Payne could have waited for him, but Greg had waved him off, and Payne didn't want to look like he was hovering, even though he was a bit. By now he was comfortable with the people who trained with him and the trainers, but Greg was still his security blanket. They'd been through so much together that it was hard for Payne to be in this kind of situation without him.

"Do you think we're lying?" he asked.

"Maybe? I guess we were all surprised because you guys are so young."

"You know as well as I do that we don't choose when we

meet our mates."

"I mean, yeah, but you could have waited to bond."

"My mate and I aren't bonded yet," Payne confessed. "We met not long before I started training here."

"Yet you already live with him?" Kerwin asked.

Since it was Kerwin, every person who trained with Payne and Greg would know about this conversation by the time it was over. Payne had never met someone who spread information the way Kerwin did. Payne didn't think he'd say anything if he asked him not to, but his relationship with Rob wasn't a secret.

"It's complicated. Greg and I live with our acquired family, and one of them is sick. Rob's a doctor who moved in with us to help him, which is how we ended up living together. We hadn't met before he moved in, and since he's not done helping Jasper, he's not going to leave anytime soon."

Kerwin slowly nodded. Payne could almost see the cogs turning in his brain. Kerwin was one of the most intelligent people he'd ever met, excluding Rob. He suspected the two of them would get along quite well, even though, on the surface, it seemed impossible. Kerwin was happy-go-lucky and a fighter. Rob was grumpy and wouldn't hurt a fly. Yet sometimes, they thought in similar ways, so much that it startled Payne.

"Why don't you tell us more about your mate?" Kerwin eventually asked.

"Why do you want to know more about him? So you can tell everyone else?"

Kerwin grinned. "Exactly. Now, spill the beans."

Payne didn't mind telling them about Rob, even though he'd have to be careful about what kind of information he talked about. That was fine. After four years, he was used to being careful about what he said. He felt this conversation was important to their friendship, and that was enough to convince him to talk.

Once again, Rob couldn't focus. It was becoming a common occurrence since he'd met Payne, although he had to admit that things had settled down over the past few weeks. He had a hard time believing he'd been living with the assassins for almost three months now and that he'd known Payne for two and a half months.

They were taking things slowly, but it felt right. Rob had been panicking that he'd mess things up and send Payne running, but Payne wasn't going anywhere so far. It was kind of surprising—a relief—but it also worried Rob. Payne was extremely patient with him, but eventually, he'd get annoyed. Rob didn't want to push him all the way there, but he wasn't sure what to do to avoid it. He wanted to do something nice for Payne, but he had no idea where to start.

That was why he didn't have relationships. He had no idea how to deal with them.

He scrolled down his phone, trying to find something he and Payne could do. He'd done nothing more than typing *romantic dates* in the browser, but he couldn't find anything he felt would fit him and Payne.

A dinner date night? That sounded boring, and since the website suggested doing it at home, it would also be awkward with everyone else there.

A comedy show? Rob found them irritating, and more often than not, he didn't laugh at the same things the others laughed at.

Getting a couples' tattoo? Just the thought made Rob shudder in horror. He didn't care what others did with their bodies, but he didn't like needles, not even needles he could barely see. He'd tried getting a tattoo once when he was younger, and he'd fainted when the artist had started the machine.

Plan a weekend away? That wouldn't be possible between Rob's work and Payne's training.

Wine tasting tour? That was out, since Payne was only twenty. Rent a rowboat? Unless they both wanted to drown, it was better not to do that.

Rob groaned and dropped his forehead to his desk. How was he supposed to show Payne he cared when he had no idea how to do it?

"I'm pretty sure you still need that brain," Jasper said from the open infirmary door.

The door was always open in case someone needed help, but since Rob had arrived, he'd only seen a few occurrences. Even when the assassins went on missions, they tended to come back unharmed and in one piece. It was impressive and a sign that they were good at their jobs, something Rob tried not to think too much about.

"What are you doing here?" he asked, turning his chair around so he could look at Jasper. "Did we have an appointment I forgot about?"

Jasper walked into the infirmary, shaking his head. "No. I just wanted to see you."

Rob blinked. "Why?"

Jasper cocked his head. "Because we're friends?"

"We are?" Rob supposed they were, in a way, even though they'd started as a patient-doctor relationship. Not that Rob was a real doctor, at least not one of those who worked in hospitals. That was Rocco.

"I'm offended," Jasper said. He hopped onto the bed closest to Rob's desk. "I thought we were friends."

"We are," Rob quickly said. He didn't have so many friends that he could afford to lose one.

"Then why don't you tell me what's going on? You're frustrated."

Rob narrowed his eyes. "You're trying to guilt me into telling you."

Jasper grinned. "It'll be easier if you just tell me."

Rob wasn't sure that was the case, but he supposed he could talk to Jasper. Jasper was mated, after all. He probably knew better than Rob ever could how to seduce his mate. "I want to do something nice for Payne."

"So you're planning a date?"

"I *want* to plan one. I just have no idea how to do so. I can't remember the last time I went on a date, and when I did, the other guy chose the restaurant." Rob took off his glasses and massaged the bridge of his nose.

He was tired, and trying to do this on top of everything else might not be a good idea. But he'd promised himself he wouldn't neglect Payne, and he had every intention of keeping that promise. If things between them weren't going to work, Rob didn't want the reason behind it to be that he couldn't step away from his work enough to organize a date.

"Okay, so you want to spend time alone with Payne. It needs to be a place where both of you are comfortable and where you won't have to deal with other people."

"I don't think any of the date suggestions I found fit those details."

"Do I want to know what dates you were looking into?"

"Probably not."

Jasper nodded as if he agreed. "Well, why don't you organize a picnic date on the roof?"

Rob blinked and thought about it. It sounded like a good idea, although he had some reservations. "Isn't the roof a public place? I mean, most of the people who live here spend time there, right?"

"They do, but as long as you warn them that the roof will be occupied, they'll leave you alone. It's where Frazer and I had our first date, and no one bothered us."

That made sense. Jasper and Frazer had met when Jasper was freed from the lab where he'd been experimented on. Even after he was freed, he hadn't been able to leave the warehouse because of the state he was in. He'd had trouble with his heightened strength and speed, and he didn't look quite human anymore. That hadn't stopped him and Frazer from getting together, and Rob wasn't surprised to find out they'd had a date on the roof.

"It's the best idea I've seen so far, but I'm still not quite sure where to start."

Jasper leaned closer. "Well, what do you like?"

"My job. Payne."

Jasper grinned. "I'm glad you like those things, but I meant, what do you like when it comes to dates?"

Rob threw his hands in the air. "I already told you I have no idea what I'm doing."

Jasper nodded and hopped off the bed. "Let's go."

Rob scrambled to follow him out of the infirmary. He pushed his glasses back on his nose so he wouldn't bump into anything and wished he'd had time to take off his white coat. "Where are we going?"

"Finding Graham. Since he's the cook, you're going to have to talk to him about the food. We'll have enough time to put something together for tonight if you do so now."

"Tonight?" Rob squeaked.

Jasper peered at him. "Why wait?"

"Well, Payne will be tired after his day at training."

"He trains almost every day. Do you want to wait an entire week to have this date with him? Or do you want him to feel loved and cared for tonight?"

Rob scowled at him. "Fine. We can have the date tonight." It wouldn't change anything, anyway. He and Payne had been spending every evening together, usually on the couch, watching TV or talking, surrounded by other people. They'd gotten to know each other that way, although they mostly talked about things they didn't mind the others hearing. Not that they had many secrets. Rob knew what had happened to Payne when he was a child and how he'd grown up, and Payne knew about Rob's mother.

"What's this about a date?" Armand asked, suddenly popping up in front of them and almost giving Rob a heart attack. How did the assassins *do* that?

Rob scowled at him, too, but he'd been trying to get on Armand's good side, so he quickly wiped the expression from his face. "I'm planning a date with Payne for tonight."

Armand stared at Rob for a moment. Things were still tense between them, but surely Armand had to see that Rob was doing everything he could to make Payne happy.

Eventually, Armand nodded. "Okay. You can take him on a date."

"You do realize Payne is twenty and doesn't need your authorization, right?"

"He doesn't, but I'm sure he'd like my blessing. It wouldn't be good if I told him I don't think you're good enough for him."

Since Rob still wasn't sure he was good enough for Payne, it wasn't anything he hadn't already told himself.

"But you've been treating him right," Armand admitted. "And I'm excited that my baby is going on his first real date."

"Your . . . baby?"

"Payne might not be my son by blood, but he *is* my son in spirit." Armand leaned closer.

His features flickered, an odd thing that Rob had learned Armand did on purpose to unsettle him. He was a human shifter, and he could take whatever appearance he wanted. He seemed to prefer the one he was wearing now, with the many tattoos and piercings, and Rob was glad for that. It would be awkward to never recognize him.

"But if you hurt him, I'll kill you, and I can do it in a way that will look like an accident," Armand continued.

"I won't hurt him on purpose, ever," Rob promised.

Armand stared at him for a while longer until Rob wanted to run away. Was Armand imagining all the ways he could kill him? Rob wouldn't be surprised.

Just as he expected Armand to try to strangle him, Armand grinned widely. "Good. Now let's go upstairs. I'll help you with your date."

Rob blinked and looked at Jasper, who shrugged. He didn't have time to tell Armand that he didn't need his help for the date. Armand grabbed his wrist and pulled him along, and the only thing Rob could do was follow him.

What had just happened?

As much as Payne loved Greg and the people he spent his days with, he was always glad when he arrived home. The warehouse and the people who lived there made him feel safe and like he didn't have to obsess over what he was saying. He trusted them with his life, but the same couldn't be said with the people they were training with, at least not yet. Eventually, if they were going to be council assassins together, they'd have to trust each other. For now, they were just good friends, and while Payne loved having the opportunity to spend time with them as they trained, he was also exhausted, both physically and mentally.

And the week had just started.

"I can't wait to get into bed," Greg said as they followed Dasha out of the shimmering room.

"A shower first sounds good, but I don't know if I have the energy to stand in the stall."

"A bath, then."

Payne was relieved Greg knew precisely how he felt and

that he wasn't going through this alone. It was good to have his best friend by his side as they both had this new experience.

"I might fall asleep in the bath," Greg said with a whine.

He then elbowed Payne in the ribs. Payne blinked at him, wondering what was up, and Greg tilted his chin toward the end of the hallway.

Rob stood there, looking incredibly awkward. For once, he wasn't wearing his white coat. He also wasn't wearing the huge hoodies he usually had on when he wasn't working. They were so big they swallowed his slim frame, but he loved to cuddle into them, and Payne knew they made him feel warm.

But tonight, Rob was wearing a button-down shirt and a pair of dress pants. He'd skipped the tie, but that didn't make him look any less edible. Payne stared for far longer than was acceptable, until Greg elbowed him again.

"I'm going to find Evan," Greg declared.

"I'll see you later," Payne told him.

"I don't know about that. It looks like your mate has plans for you."

That was probably true. Rob clearly had something on his mind, and Payne was suddenly not so tired anymore. He wanted to find out what was going on, so he sauntered to his mate. Greg walked past them with a wave, and as soon as he'd disappeared around the corner, Payne grabbed Rob's waist and pulled him close.

Rob squeaked, but he wrapped his arms around Payne's neck and kissed him back when Payne leaned closer.

"Welcome home," Rob said in a warm voice. "Did you have a good day?"

"It's perfect now that I have you in my arms."

Rob's cheeks flushed, but he seemed pleased. Payne was starting to realize that not many people had done that for Rob.

He'd barely talked about the guys he'd dated, but Payne knew enough to know they'd been disasters. Those people hadn't understood Rob the way Payne did, and while it made Payne want to hunt them down for hurting his mate, their loss was his gain. Rob deserved to have someone who took care of him the way he took care of everyone else. A lot rested on his shoulders, and between the work he was doing with Jasper and his mother, Payne wanted to take care of him.

"You should go to shower," Rob said.

"Do I stink so badly?" Payne teased.

To his surprise, Rob leaned closer and pressed his nose against the side of Payne's neck. He took a deep breath, which made Payne shudder in pleasure. Gosh, the things he wanted to do to his mate.

But so far, they hadn't done more than kissing. They were cautious around each other, almost afraid to take things further in case they didn't work out as a couple. Payne was starting to get over that fear, especially now that he knew that in the beginning, Rob had rejected him because he thought he wasn't good enough. Sometimes, Payne suspected he still felt that way.

He'd do whatever he could to show Rob that wasn't true.

"You smell of you, and while it's not unpleasant, I suspect you'd feel better if you got a shower," Rob said.

"I'll go upstairs. Do you know what Graham cooked for dinner?"

Rob shuffled his feet. He was a fidgety person in general, but it seemed odd in this situation, enough that Payne wondered what was going on. Was Rob hiding something?

Payne's mind went straight to the fact that maybe Rob wanted to break up with him. Maybe he was hiding the fact that he didn't want to be with Payne.

No. If Rob was hiding something like that, he wouldn't have kissed Payne. They wouldn't be wrapped in each other's arms right now. Payne had to remember that and stop letting the little voice in the back of his head that always told him he wasn't good enough convince him that wasn't the case.

"I have no idea," Rob said. "But I have a surprise for you."

"A good one, I hope?"

"Would I give you a bad surprise?"

"I sure hope not."

"It's nothing bad, I promise. Just, please, can you go shower and wear something comfortable?"

Payne took a step back and looked Rob up and down. "Only if you wear something comfortable, too."

"I wanted to look good for you." Rob smoothed down the shirt over his stomach. "These are the nicest clothes I brought."

Payne cupped Rob's cheek and kissed him gently. "You look incredibly gorgeous, whatever you wear. If I have to put on comfortable clothes, so do you."

Rob hesitated, but only for a few seconds. Then he nodded. "All right. I'll go change, and I'll meet you on the roof."

Where had that come from? "The roof?"

"Yes."

"Shouldn't we have dinner first? We can go to the roof once we're done eating, but I'm kind of hungry."

Rob crossed his arms over his chest and glared. "Can you just let me do this and go along with it?"

Payne grinned. So Rob *was* hiding something. Payne would find out what it was once he went along with Rob's plans, so he nodded. "All right. I'll meet you on the roof in about twenty minutes. Is that okay?"

"It is," Rob agreed.

Payne didn't want to let him go, but they both had things to do, so after one last kiss, he strode down the hallway. He was tempted to look back to make sure Rob was still there, but he didn't. Rob wasn't going anywhere. Slowly, they were making things work between them, and that was perfectly fine with Payne. He didn't care if it took them years to be secure in their relationship the way Greg and Evan were. It had been years for them, after all. But Payne and Rob had something good going on, and Payne was fine taking things as slow as they both needed to. He didn't need a whirlwind romance. He just needed Rob, and that wasn't the kind of person Rob was.

He whistled as he made his way upstairs to his room. Rob was nowhere to be seen, but he'd have to come upstairs eventually. Maybe they could go up to the roof together. Whatever Rob was hiding, Payne was excited to find out now. The fear was gone, which was good because Payne didn't want to be afraid when it came to Rob.

Payne suspected it would take a long time for the voice in his head to finally shut up. It wasn't a good voice, and he tried not to listen to it, especially since it sounded like the first woman who'd bought him. But sometimes Payne had a hard time ignoring it.

He'd have to work harder on that. He didn't want to mess things up with Rob, and he wanted to be happy. He *deserved* to be happy. After what he'd been through, life was finally looking up. He had a great family, a comfortable home, a job he was looking forward to starting, and his mate.

What more could he want?

Rob couldn't remember the last time he'd been so nervous. Thanks to Jasper and Armand, he had everything ready, but he still felt like it wasn't enough. He wanted tonight to be perfect because it was what Payne deserved, but he wasn't sure that what he'd done was adequate.

He stared at the nest—there was no other word for it—he and Jasper had put together. They'd had a good base with the comfortable couches on the roof, and Rob had chosen the one under the gazebo Payne had dragged him to that one time. He'd mentioned liking this spot especially, and it was hidden enough that even if someone came upstairs, they wouldn't notice them as long as they weren't noisy.

Jasper had told Rob he'd spread the news that the roof was occupied, and he'd promised everyone would stay away. Rob hoped that would work. He didn't know what would happen between him and Payne, but just in case, he didn't want them to have spectators, even by mistake.

He and Jasper had covered the couch with pillows and blankets. It was one of those sectional couches, so they'd be able to stretch out and look at the stars since they'd moved it to the edge of the gazebo. The weather was cooperating, and the sky was clear, even though it was cold. Rob supposed it would give them an excuse to snuggle together, although he wasn't sure they'd need one.

Along with the blankets and pillows, there was food and drinks on the table Rob had dragged closer. Graham had gone all out and prepared an array of tiny sandwiches and finger foods. He'd been almost as excited as Rob about the date, which Rob had found puzzling until Graham had told him that he and the others had watched Payne grow up over the past four years. He'd gone from a terrified teenager to a strong young man, and they were all happy he'd found his mate and that he was happy. It was kind of scary to think that everyone was watching them to make sure Rob treated Payne the way he deserved, but since he had no intention of ever hurting Payne deliberately, it didn't matter.

"Rob?" Payne called out from the roof door.

Rob swallowed and rushed to him. He didn't want Payne to see the surprise just yet. When he reached Payne, he was relieved to find him hovering by the still open door. Payne beamed when he saw Rob, and Rob found himself smiling back.

"I wasn't sure you'd be up here yet," Payne said.

Rob pulled him into his arms and kissed him. He'd never cared much about kissing, and with his exes, he'd always been distracted. There was always something more interesting to think about, like his job, but he'd never felt that way with Payne. Maybe it was because Payne was his mate—he was perfect for Rob, and Rob couldn't have ignored him even if he'd tried. When he was with him, he didn't want to think about work or anything that wasn't Payne.

Payne was still smiling when the kiss ended. "Not that I'm complaining, but what's this about? Because I'm starving."

"Don't worry. I have food for you." Rob cleared his throat. "This is a date."

Payne's smile widened. "Really?"

"Really. I hope you'll like it."

Payne pressed a quick kiss to Rob's lips. "I'll love it."

"You don't even know what I organized."

"Doesn't matter. You did this thinking of me, and that's all that matters."

Rob wasn't sure that was right, but it didn't matter. He took Payne's hand and guided him toward the gazebo. Payne was wearing a pair of sweatpants and a soft long-sleeved t-shirt, which mirrored the clothes Rob had thrown on after Payne had ordered him to change. He'd wanted to look good for Payne, but he couldn't deny it would be better to snuggle under the blankets wearing comfy pants.

"It's not much," he warned. "But I wanted to do something for you, and I thought you'd rather stay home after a day of training."

"You're not wrong, and it's perfect."

Payne flopped onto the couch and sighed in pleasure. Rob felt a bit ridiculous, but he pulled the blankets around Payne, cocooning him before turning his attention to the food. He put together a plate of a little bit of everything, handed it to his mate, then quickly did the same for himself.

They sat in silence for a while, the only sounds the ones they made as they ate. Rob wasn't sure what to say, and he didn't want to interrupt Payne as he ate, so he felt it was safer to keep his mouth shut. He had no idea what he was doing, anyway. He'd probably manage to fuck things up if he said anything.

"I needed that," Payne said when he was done eating. He'd reclined against the couch and was staring at the sky, his hands linked over his stomach.

Rob was a bit tense, but having eaten and being with Payne helped him relax. Even if he did fuck things up like he expected, Payne wouldn't care. He'd probably laugh it off, then help Rob fix whatever stupid thing he'd done or said.

"How was your day?" Rob eventually asked to fill the silence. It felt ridiculous to ask something so mundane, but he had to start somewhere.

"Tough but satisfying." Payne rolled to his side, facing Rob, and Rob did the same. "It's good to know I'm finally doing something, you know?"

They snuggled under the blankets, so close their chests brushed against each other and their legs tangled. "Even before you started this, you were doing something," Rob said.

"Yeah, but not like this. I graduated high school, but I was late doing that."

"So? You had extenuating circumstances."

"I know. But I feel good finally doing something I've wanted for a while. The assassins saved Greg and me, and I can never thank them enough for that. I guess I want to show them it wasn't all for nothing."

"They already know that." Rob disliked when Payne spoke about himself as if he wasn't good enough. "And I do, too. You're perfect, whatever you decide to do."

Payne's smile was gentle and soft. "So are you."

Rob wasn't so sure about that, but it didn't matter. As long as Payne thought he was perfect and wanted him, he was happy.

They moved at the same time, their lips reaching for each other. Payne sighed against Rob's mouth and deepened the kiss. Rob had no idea what he wanted, but he was willing to give him everything.

"I'm falling in love with you," he found himself whispering.

Payne's eyes widened.

Rob wanted to run and never face Payne again, but Payne kissed him again before he could.

"Me, too," Payne said between kisses. "I'm falling for you, and I don't understand how it happened so fast, but I don't care. I just know I want to be with you."

"I'm awkward and messy, and I forget meals and birthdays and appointments. I spend most of my days focused on work or on my mother, and I know I'm not ugly, but I'm nowhere near as gorgeous as you. You could do so much better." Rob truly believed that.

Payne caught Rob's cheeks with his hands. "I can't do better, Rob. You're my mate. That means *you're* the best for me, and I truly believe that."

Rob nodded, because what else could he do? He wanted Payne to believe that and to never let him go. He'd do whatever he had to in order to make sure that didn't happen, but in case he failed, at least he'd have had this—the time spent with Payne under the stars, wrapped around each other.

To his surprise, Payne rolled them until Rob was under him. Rob briefly wondered if he shouldn't be the one to take charge since he was older, but then Payne kissed him, and he stopped caring. His legs fell apart as if they had a mind of their own, and Payne settled between them.

Rob hadn't wanted to assume anything like this would happen. In fact, he'd been terrified at the thought that it might. He'd never been great in bed—his few exes all agreed on that—and he didn't want to send Payne running. But with Payne, it was almost easy to forget about the fears and focus instead on what they were doing, especially when Payne rolled his hips and Rob felt how hard he already was.

"Tell me what you want," Payne said with a growl that sent shivers down Rob's spine.

"Just you, whatever you want to give me."

Payne shook his head and caught Rob's earlobe with his teeth. He gently pulled, and Rob wasn't sure whether to lean into it or lean back. "Tell me. I need to know what you're ready for." He hesitated. "I'm not sure we should go all the way tonight. I mean, I want to, and this is the perfect date, but I feel you're not quite ready."

With a puff of breath, Rob relaxed. "I'm not." Payne would never treat him the way his exes had, but the fear was still there. Rob wasn't entirely at ease, and it was good to know that Payne wouldn't push.

Payne kissed him as if he'd only been waiting for Rob's agreement. It was clear that hadn't been enough to dissuade him from doing whatever they were about to do, for which Rob was grateful. He felt a bit like a teenager who was just discovering sex, and in a way, he was. Sex had never been like this with anyone else.

Payne pressed harder against Rob, making him keen. Rob pressed his head back into the pillow, and Payne took advantage of the position to kiss down his throat. It felt impossible, but Rob already felt like he was about to explode—and like he was about to cry. No one had ever taken care of him this way, and he had no idea how to deal with the feelings it created in him.

"Let go," Payne murmured against Rob's neck. "I'll catch

you. I promise."

Rob believed him, so he obeyed. He screwed his eyes shut and did what Payne had asked, letting go. He let Payne catch him, and it felt so damn good. Rob hadn't expected anything like this to happen tonight, but he wouldn't change it for anything in the world. He'd made himself vulnerable, had taken a risk, but Payne hadn't betrayed him.

Rob couldn't imagine his life without him, not anymore.

He felt Payne shudder above him and blinked his eyes open. Payne's expression was contorted, and Rob realized he was coming.

He'd been the one who did that. He'd made Payne come, and maybe he'd caught Payne just like Payne had caught him.

They were different, and Rob had thought it meant they couldn't work. But they seemed to fill in things that were missing in the other, and maybe that was why they were mates. Payne took care of Rob, even though he was younger — young enough to be Rob's son if he'd had him at eighteen, but Rob tried not to think about that. And Rob, well, he was there for Payne when Payne needed him.

That was all he could do. He was a disaster in most aspects of his life, but he wanted to succeed in this.

And he would.

CHAPTER FIVE

Payne flopped on the damp grass. He was breathing hard, but he grinned when Greg sat next to him. He raised his fist, and Greg bumped his against it.

"Great job," Greg said.

"You, too."

They were used to training together, which meant today wasn't the first time they had to fight each other. When they did it at home, the assassins usually took bets on who would win. They were evenly matched when it came to strength, and while Greg was larger, Payne was faster. Sometimes Greg won, and other times Payne did.

Payne had won today.

He rolled to his side and grabbed his backpack, dragging his water bottle out of it. He sat up and took a drink, and as he did so, his phone caught his attention. The screen had lit up with a text message, and it allowed him to see that Jasper had called him three times and texted him twice.

Payne frowned and took out his phone. They weren't supposed to look at their phones while they were training, but since they weren't children, no one took them away. Most of the others left her phone in their dorm rooms, but since Greg and Payne didn't live here, they kept theirs in their backpacks.

"Payne!" Jamison thundered. "What are you doing with that phone?"

In any other circumstance, Payne would have put it away and apologized, but he was reading Jasper's text, and as he did so, he got to his feet.

"Payne!" Jamison said again. He stormed toward Payne, and Payne finally turned his attention to him. "I apologize," he said before Jamison could start yelling at him. "It's an emergency."

That gave Jamison pause. "Is it?"

Payne turned his phone so Jamison could see the text Jasper had sent him. "Jasper's a friend. Rob is my mate."

The text was short and straightforward, but it still terrified Payne.

Rob got a call about his mother taking a fall and had to rush to her. Call him.

Payne swallowed. "My mate's mother has dementia."

Jamison's expression softened. "And you need to go to him."

"I can stay if I have to, but I'd rather be with him and his mother, at least for today. I need to know what happened to her."

"I don't expect you to stay when you have a family emergency. Go."

Payne put his phone into his pocket and grabbed his backpack. Greg patted his shoulder, silently telling him that he was there if he needed anything. Payne nodded, relieved as always to have his friend, but when he moved toward building E, he realized he hadn't called Dasha.

"Seymour will take you," Jamison declared loud enough that Payne saw Seymour turn their way.

Payne wasn't sure it was a good idea, but he didn't want to waste time, so he nodded.

Seymour looked way too excited to be able to leave, even if only for a moment. He was sweating, and his face was tomato red. He bounced toward Payne, but his expression changed when he realized something had happened.

"Everything okay?" he asked.

"I don't know yet. My mate's mother fell, and she has dementia."

"So that's why Jamison wants me to take you wherever you need to go."

Payne nodded. "I'm sorry to take you away from training. I could call someone else."

"It's fine. Vivian was kicking my ass, anyway."

They had to walk to building E, since the rest of the facility was shielded against unwanted shimmerings. As soon as they were inside, Payne grabbed Seymour's hand. Seymour squeezed it, still looking worried. "All right?" he asked.

"I'll feel better once I'm with my mate."

"Just focus on him, all right?"

Payne closed his eyes and thought of Rob. It was easy, especially now that they'd become closer. He was surprised Rob hadn't tried calling him, but he also understood. Rob had been alone for so long, and he was used to taking care of his mother on his own. It probably hadn't occurred to him that Payne would want to know that something had happened so he could be there for Rob and help him. They'd have to talk about that, but not right now.

When Payne opened his eyes, they were in a room that was nothing like the one they'd just left. The walls were painted a light blue, and some of the tiles on the floor were chipped. It was empty, but several chairs lined the walls, telling him it was a waiting area. The door stood open, and he could see they were in what looked like a hospital.

"I didn't want to shimmer you directly to him in case we interrupted something," Seymour explained. "But he's in the next room."

Payne nodded and left the room. He peeked into the next one, and it couldn't have been any different. It was cozy and almost looked like a normal bedroom you'd find in an apartment. A few things pointed to the fact that it wasn't, including medical equipment, like the bed on which a woman was stretched out. Rob was sitting next to her, talking, but he looked up when he heard Payne.

His eyes widened, and he shot to his feet. "What are you doing here?" he asked as he rushed to Payne's side.

"Jasper texted me that they called you about your mother. How is she?"

Rob looked back at her. She was staring at the TV now, not one bit interested in what was happening between them. Her gray hair was neatly combed, and she was wearing a white sweater. She'd stretched out on top of the covers, so Payne could see she was also wearing black pants and white socks. She looked fine, but what did Payne know?

"She's okay," Rob whispered.

"Are you sure?"

Rob nodded, and he looked like he wanted to say more, but just then, a doctor arrived. She looked from Rob to Payne, clearly curious, but now wasn't the time to explain who Payne was. He quickly squeezed Rob's hand, then gently pushed him toward the doctor. "It looks like she's here for your mother."

"You're leaving?" Rob sounded like he wasn't happy about that.

"Not if you don't want me to."

"I don't."

"Then I'll stay. You go and talk to the doctor, and I'll be right outside the room."

Rob stared for a moment before nodding. Payne kissed him, unable to stay away, then quickly stepped out. The doctor walked in, thankfully not saying anything.

When Payne turned, it was to find Seymour staring at him. He hadn't even realized Seymour had stuck around, but he should have. What kind of council assassin would he be if he wasn't even aware of his surroundings?

"So that's your mate," Seymour said.

Payne nodded. He was glad Seymour had stayed. If he

hadn't, Payne would be pacing the hallway, and he doubted anyone would be happy with him.

"I'll admit I thought he was closer to your age," Seymour continued.

Payne glared at him. "If you're going to criticize my mate, you can leave."

Seymour grinned. "Sorry. It was just an observation, not a critique. I should probably go anyway, but I wanted to make sure everything was okay and that you were all right first."

Seymour had been teasing. Payne should have realized that, and he would have if he hadn't been so overwhelmed and worried. He might not have known Seymour long, but the Nix was a friend, and Payne was grateful that he'd brought him here.

"Sorry," he murmured.

"Don't worry about it. Let me know if you need me to come and pick you up. I'll take you wherever you have to go, including home."

"I'll let you know if I need help, but I don't think I will. I think I'll take Rob straight home once we're done here. He won't want to meet anyone new, or I'd have introduced you."

"I didn't expect to be introduced to him when his mother is hurt. We can do it some other day."

And they would. Payne had been wary initially because he hadn't known the other trainees, but he trusted them. He wanted both sides of his life to mix and become one, and that meant introducing the trainees to the assassins and Rob. He'd have to ask Win, and he was ready to do that, but not right now.

Right now, he needed to focus on Rob and his mother.

"How are we doing?" the doctor asked as she stopped beside Rob's mother's bed.

Rob's mother didn't give her any attention. She kept staring at the screen, and while Rob really wanted to talk to the doctor, he didn't want to leave his mother alone. She didn't like doctors, and he didn't blame her for that. "She's fine, as far as I can see," he said.

The doctor smiled. She was young and not someone Rob had dealt with before. She'd taken care of his mother when she'd fallen, and he was grateful for it, even though it was her job. "That's good. Do you think we could talk for a moment?"

"I don't want to leave her alone."

"I can stay with her," a familiar voice said from the open door.

Rob turned to look at Payne. He was alone now, which hopefully meant his friend was gone. It wasn't that Rob didn't want to meet Payne's friends or that he wasn't happy that Payne had them. This just wasn't the right moment for him to be distracted from his mom.

"I can't ask that of you," Rob said.

Payne looked from Rob to the doctor, then stepped into the room. "You're not asking. I'm offering. I realize this isn't the nicest way for me to meet your mom, but it'll be fine."

Rob was still hesitating, but his mother seemed so focused on the TV that she probably wouldn't even notice he was gone, let alone that she'd never met Payne. Even if she did, she'd probably think she'd met him and forgotten.

He got to his feet. "Thank you," he murmured.

Payne's smile was gentle. "Don't worry about it. Go with the doctor and hear what she has to say. Your mother and I will be here when you get back."

That much was true. Rob's mother wasn't going anywhere, especially after she'd fallen.

Thankfully, the fall had only resulted in a few bruises and scratches. She hadn't hit her head or broken anything, which was a relief. When Rob had gotten the phone call from the home, he'd expected the worst.

He followed the doctor outside the door. They stopped just outside of the room, where Rob was able to see Payne sit in the chair he'd just vacated. The doctor cleared her throat, getting his attention, so he turned to look at her. "I apologize," he said.

She smiled. "It's quite all right. I understand you're worried about your mother. Is it the first time she's met your partner?"

"He's my mate, but yes."

"Oh. Congratulations."

He could see she was curious, probably because of the difference in age between him and Payne, but thankfully, she didn't ask questions. He wouldn't have been sure how to answer, and he wouldn't have wanted to try, anyway. What was between him and Payne was only their business and no one else's.

"Thank you. I assume you're here to tell me that my mother will be fine?"

The doctor straightened. Rob was sure she'd told him her name, but he'd been focused on his mom, and he couldn't remember it. "Yes. The last test results came back, and she's okay. As you noticed, she has a few bruises, but nothing worse."

Rob finally allowed himself to relax. "What happened?"

"From what I was told, they were walking in the garden when another patient needed help. The nurse who was walking with your mother went there for a moment, and your mother stumbled. A root, probably."

Rob's instinct was to rage. He'd selected this place because he'd thought his mother would be protected, yet she hadn't been. But he realized that unless he hired a personal nurse for his mother, he'd have to learn to deal with this. These people did their best to keep their patients safe and happy, and Rob knew how hard that was. He'd had a hard time dealing with his mother, and there was only one of her. He couldn't imagine what it was like to have to deal with so many patients.

He remembered when he'd wanted to keep her at home with him. She'd been the one who convinced him she needed a place like this one for the times when she wasn't lucid. She'd begged him to let her go, and eventually, he had. He hadn't had a choice, no matter how much he wished he had. She'd needed more help than he could give her. He'd been afraid that she'd manage to sneak out when he was at work, even though he'd hired a nurse. This was the best outcome for both of them, but sometimes he still wondered.

"We apologize for what happened," the doctor said.

"It's all right. I know how hard the nurses work."

"I'll make sure your mother's regular doctor has all the information about what happened today."

Rob was glad to be able to step away. Now that he was reassured and knew his mom would be fine, he wanted to spend time with her. He wasn't sure it would be possible today because she was a bit shaken, but he could sit next to her bed and just be there.

He said goodbye to the doctor but hesitated before going in. He had no idea what he'd find when he went into the room, and it was honestly terrifying. His mom was probably still watching TV, so he sucked in a breath and walked into the room, closing the door behind himself before turning around.

He'd chosen this place for a reason. He earned more than enough money thanks to his research and the fact that the council was paying him handsomely to help Jasper. He was also lucky that his parents had been wealthy, so he'd been able to pick a facility that would allow his mother to have a personal bedroom that looked more like her room at home than a hospital room. There were signs that this was a care facility, but he thought his mother was happy here. She wasn't always easy to understand, so he hoped he was right. He also hoped his mother was comfortable and that he wouldn't have to move her. Finding this place had been a hassle. Most of these facilities had a waiting list as long as Rob's arm.

When he turned to face his mother and Payne, he was stunned to see that his mother wasn't watching TV anymore. Payne had moved the chair closer to her bed, and they were talking, their heads close together. It was almost as if they'd known each other for years, and Rob couldn't look away.

His mother was smiling.

He couldn't remember the last time she'd smiled like that. She looked like her old self, and the sight made his chest feel tight. He wasn't jealous that Payne had been able to do it. He was just happy that his mom was okay.

Payne looked up when he heard Rob move closer. He grinned, then turned back to Rob's mother. "I told you that you didn't have to worry about us becoming friends," he said.

"Why on earth were you worried about me meeting this nice young man?" Rob's mother asked.

Rob stared, wondering if she was lucid. It looked like it, but he didn't want to hope, just in case. "Well, you just took a fall," he explained.

His mother waved his words away. "I'm fine. It was just a tumble."

"I'm glad to hear that. So, Payne, have you explained who you are and why you're here to meet my mom?"

Payne's cheeks flushed. "Not really. I told her I was a friend of yours. I wasn't sure what you'd want me to tell her."

"The truth." Rob moved to the other side of the bed and took one of his mother's hands. "Mom, this is Payne. He's my mate. Payne, this is my mother, Hyacinth."

"That's a beautiful name," Payne said.

Rob's mother *giggled.*

Rob stared at her, unable to wrap his mind around what was happening.

"Thank you," she said. "So you're my son's mate?"

Her words startled Rob. She knew he was her son, then. He hadn't been sure, and it was good to find out that even though she might not remember this, she was meeting Payne as herself. There was no way to know how long it would last, but that was fine. Rob would deal with it when it ended.

Payne and Rob's mother continued talking, but Rob stayed out of the conversation. It felt good to listen to them, and he was perfectly fine doing so however long they wanted to talk.

Payne liked Rob's mother. Sometimes, he could see moments when she wasn't entirely there and was confused, but it didn't last long. At least for today, it gave Rob and his mother the opportunity to be together, which was all Payne wanted.

When a nurse knocked on the door, the three of them looked up. She smiled. "Hyacinth, I heard you took a fall?"

"She's fine," Rob said.

"I *am* fine and able to answer for myself," his mother snarked.

Instead of getting angry, Rob grinned. "I apologize."

"It's fine, but why don't you go with Angela to get some tea? I'm quite thirsty, and I'm sure Payne could do with a few cookies." She leaned closer to Payne. "I'd offer you coffee, but they won't let me have it."

Luckily, the nurse laughed. "That's right. The last thing we need is the bunch of you hyped up on caffeine. Rob, do you want to come with me? I can give you a tray."

Payne got to his feet, too. He wanted a few moments alone with Rob to check if he was okay, but he wasn't sure they should leave Rob's mother on her own. When he looked at her, she waved him away. "I'll be fine for a few minutes."

"Are you sure?"

"Of course. Go with my son." She leaned closer. "I was fine before, too. I just didn't want to talk to the doctor, so I stared at the TV." Payne grinned. Rob was already by the door talking to the nurse, but Payne still hesitated. To his surprise, Rob's mother grabbed his hand. "Be there for my son, please. I know that most of the time when he comes to visit me, I'm not myself. I try my best to be there for him when I am, but he needs more people. I won't be here forever."

"Of course you will," Payne murmured.

She laughed. "I wish I could be, but it's fine. I lived my life, and it was a happy one. I always worry about Rob, so I'm glad he found you."

"I'm glad I found him, too."

"The two of you needed each other. That's why you met."

Payne suspected she was right. Some people thought there was a reason why mates met when they did, but Payne had never given it much thought. Maybe there was something to it, but in the end, it didn't matter when he and Rob had met. It just mattered that they had.

Rob had already disappeared through the door, so Payne hurried to catch up with him. When he did, it was to find Rob at the nurses' station, still talking to Angela.

"She's been herself since this morning when she woke up," the nurse was saying. "I was going to call you anyway because I know you like to come when she's lucid. She wanted to see you, too, but we have everyone take a walk after breakfast, as you know."

"It's good for them to get some fresh air."

"Exactly." The nurse smiled when she noticed Payne. "Well, your partner is here. I'm sure he can help you carry everything back to the room. As long as you don't need anything else, I'll check on my other patients."

"We'll be fine, thank you," Rob reassured her.

Payne took the tray from him when he tried to move toward his mother's room. It was heavy with cups, a teapot, and a plate of cookies. Payne was surprised to see the cups looked old and were decorated with flowers rather than being cheap plastic cups, but he supposed it matched the general feeling of this place. It was a medical facility, but it was also home for many people.

"You don't have to stay," Rob said as they walked back to his mother's room. "I know you were training."

"I was, but I'm done for the day. You don't have to worry."

Rob didn't look convinced. "You don't have to deal with her."

"Don't I? I mean, it's great to meet her, and she's nice, but beyond that, she's your mother, and you're my mate. It's kind of my job to make sure she's okay, too."

"You might be my mate, but she's *my* mother."

"Exactly. When we bond, she'll be my mother-in-law." Payne already considered her his mother-in-law, but he didn't know if saying it would send Rob running. They'd been taking things slow, and while the relationship was solid, sometimes, one or both of them was still hesitant. Considering their pasts, it wasn't a surprise, but they were working through it.

Rob slowly nodded. "In that case, thank you."

Payne shook his head. "You don't have to thank me. I realize she's sick, and I've been reading up on dementia."

Robert blinked. "You have?"

"I wanted to know what to expect. I'm not an expert, but I have a vague idea of what's going on and what will happen in the future. I want to be there for you both." Because it wouldn't be easy. Rob's mother wouldn't get better. She'd decline, and there was no avoiding that.

Payne hoped he was doing everything right. He had no

idea what he was doing, and no amount of reading would help him understand better. But he knew what to do to be there for Rob, and that was what he planned to do. Rob had been shouldering all of this on his own until now. It was time for him to have help, and who better than Payne to provide it?

They got back to Hyacinth's room to find her still watching TV. She smiled when she heard them, and they sat down with her to get tea. Payne let Rob take care of his mother because he had no idea how she liked her tea, and he smiled when she snatched a cookie from the plate on the tray.

"If I can't have coffee, at least I can have cookies," she said.

"Too many cookies won't do you any good," Rob pointed out.

"Who cares? I'm old. I won't last forever, anyway. I might as well enjoy my last years on this earth."

Rob paled, and Payne was glad he'd moved both the chairs to the same side of the bed so they could be closer. He quickly squeezed Rob's knee, and Rob smiled gratefully at him.

"You two are adorable together," Rob's mother said.

"I'm thirty-eight, Mom. I'm not adorable," Rob protested.

"You'll always be adorable to me, because you'll always be my baby, no matter how old you are."

Payne had no experience with mothers. He didn't think he'd ever met a mother, now that he thought about it. It was nice to watch Rob with his, and he took advantage of the time he had with them. He hoped he'd be allowed to come back and visit, but even if he wasn't, the sight of Rob with his mom warmed his chest. Even though she was ill, she loved her son with all she had. He loved her, too. It was clear in every move he made.

It wasn't fair. There were so many people out there who were abusive and hateful. Yet they had their families, and they were thriving. Then there was Rob and his mother, who loved each other but were losing the other a little more every day.

Rob knocked his shoulder against Payne's. "Everything all right?"

Payne forced himself to smile. "I'm perfect." And at that moment, he was. He wished this would never end and that Rob could have his mother back. Unfortunately, things didn't work that way, and an hour later, they had to leave. Rob's mother needed a nap, and even though she tried resisting the urge to sleep, it was time for Payne and Rob to go.

Payne stepped away from the bed to give Rob and his mother a moment on their own. He could hear them whispering to each other, and when he looked up, he noticed they were holding hands. It was sweet, and his heart ached for both of them.

Rob's mother waved Payne close again, and he went. He'd do pretty much anything she asked of him.

"It was so good to meet you," she said with a smile.

"It was. I hope you'll allow me to visit you again."

"You can come anytime you want. Rob, can you add him to the list of allowed visitors?"

"I'll do it as we leave."

"And don't feel you have to wait for Rob to visit me. You can come anytime." She hesitated. "I can't promise you'll find me like this every time you come. In fact, I can promise you that won't be the case."

"It's fine. I'll be happy to visit you."

And Payne really would be.

Rob was exhausted emotionally. His day had been emotionally heavy, but he'd have been in worse shape if he hadn't had Payne by his side. He was still surprised that Payne had come all the way here just to be with him, but as soon as they left his mother's room, he turned to Payne and threw himself at him. Payne stumbled, trying to hold both of them up, but he squeezed his arms around Rob, and Rob allowed him to take his weight, if only for a moment.

He needed it. He'd always faced these situations on his own, and it was odd not to have to. It was good, too. Rob felt just a little bit less alone, and it wasn't something he was used to. Sometimes, he still wondered what Payne saw in him and if he would stay or go, but he was starting to be convinced more and more that Payne was here to stay. It would be so much easier for him to leave and never look back. Instead, he supported Rob in a way no one ever had.

"Thank you," Rob whispered.

Payne rubbed Rob's back. "You're welcome, but you have nothing to thank me for."

Rob wanted to stay in Payne's arms forever, but they were in the hallway, and people were walking around them. They needed to get home, where they could be together. So he stepped away and walked toward the nurses' station again so he could add Payne to the list of visitors who could come in any time to see his mother. It was painfully short, with only two names as of now.

But as he did so, he couldn't help but wonder what Payne expected from him. They were going home, and they'd apparently spend the rest of the day together, but Rob wasn't up for anything physical. He wanted to have sex with Payne—in fact, he wanted to have sex with his mate all the time—but not today. Emotionally, he wasn't up for it, but Payne was young, and he hadn't had the same reaction as Rob to what had happened today. What if he got angry because Rob didn't want to have sex with him? Rob didn't want to disappoint him, but he also didn't want to do something he wasn't fully into.

"You're thinking too hard," Payne said as he grabbed Rob's hand on their way to the shimmering room.

"When have I not thought too hard?" Rob teased.

But Payne didn't smile. Instead, he shook his head. "Something's bothering you. What is it? I don't think it's your mother, but I can't quite place it."

"How do you do that?"

Payne chuckled. "Do what? Read you so well?"

"Yes."

"You're not that hard to read, Rob. You have worry written over your face."

Rob rubbed his face. He hadn't realized he was so easy to read, although he supposed if it was Payne who read him, he didn't care. They'd promised they'd try to be honest with each other, and that was what he should do. There was no use obsessing over what Payne would or wouldn't want. "I just can't wait to get home and cuddle." Because that was what Rob needed.

To his relief, Payne nodded. "We can do that. I'm not going back to training today, so I'm yours for the rest of the day."

"That's good. I just don't think I'm up for anything physical."

Payne blinked. "You mean sex?"

Rob looked around, but no one had heard them. Still, he moved closer. "Yes. Honestly, I'm still freaking out over what happened, although it's not as much the fall as it is everything else. It was good to be able to talk to my mom the way we did, and I hate that I might not get this the next time I see her. I hate her illness, and I wish there was something I could do to help her through it."

Payne dragged Rob into the shimmering room. It was empty, and Rob started taking out his phone to get a Nix, but Payne stopped him when he grabbed his wrist.

"I've already texted one of the twins. Jolyn is coming to pick us up, so you don't have to worry about that. I just wanted to take a moment to address what you just said." He looked around, but the room was empty. That seemed to satisfy him because he nodded.

"What are you doing?" Rob asked.

"I don't expect sex from you, Rob. I don't expect it now, or ever. Sure, I *want* to have sex with you, but only if it's something you want, too. Otherwise, what fun is it?"

Rob didn't know how to answer, or even if he could. His throat felt tight, and he had trouble breathing. "Thank you," he eventually croaked.

Payne cupped his cheek and gently kissed him. "Eventually, you'll have to stop thanking me. What I'm doing is perfectly normal and nothing to thank me for. This is how every single one of your exes should have treated you."

But none of them had. Rob had lucked out when it came to his mate, and he was very much aware of it.

"Oh, sorry," a voice said behind Payne.

Rob looked around him to find Jolyn staring at them. "Thank you for picking us up," he said.

"I can come back later."

Rob shook his head. "No. I want to go home."

Jolyn seemed worried, but he nodded. He took Rob's hand while Payne clung to Rob, and the three of them shimmered back home. As soon as they arrived, Payne dragged Rob along. Rob had no idea where they were going, but he didn't care. He wanted a bed, to be able to hide under the covers and never come out, or at the very least, not to come out for the rest of the day. He shouldn't be so tired, because he hadn't done much today, but he couldn't deny how he felt.

He finally realized they weren't going to his room when they entered Payne's. Even though Payne had said he didn't expect sex, the place gave Rob a moment of hesitation.

Thankfully, Payne mistook it for something else. He dropped Rob's hand and grabbed a t-shirt that had been thrown on the chair by the desk. "Sorry for the mess," he said.

Rob forced himself to relax. Payne was a straight shooter. He wouldn't tell him anything he didn't believe, which meant that when he'd said he didn't expect sex, that was the truth.

Rob watched Payne run around his bedroom, picking up dirty clothes and pushing stuff into his closet. He straightened his bed, and by the time he was done, the room looked, well, not neat, but less messy.

That was when he turned his attention to Rob. He grabbed Rob's hand and pulled him toward the bed, then pushed him onto it. He crouched in front of Rob and took off his shoes, even though Rob tried to push him away to do it himself. Payne seemed bent on protecting Rob and taking care of him, and eventually, Rob gave in. He *wanted* to be taken care of. He wanted someone to be here for him the way Payne was now and for him not to have to shoulder everything on his own. It didn't matter that Payne was young and that they'd just recently met. Payne filled a hole in Rob's life that Rob hadn't been aware was there, and Rob prayed he would never leave him.

Payne pushed Rob back on the bed once he was done with Rob's shoes and socks. Rob's eyes widened when Payne quickly unbuttoned his pants and drew them down his legs, but he kept Rob's underwear where it was. He wanted Rob to be comfortable, and that was it.

So Rob got comfortable. He took off his shirt, too, and buried himself under the blankets. He pulled them high over his head, only leaving a sliver of his face out so he could breathe. He cocooned himself in Payne's scent and the knowledge that this was his bed, and he closed his eyes.

He could hear Payne move around the room, but he didn't look to see what was happening. He wasn't surprised when he felt the bed dip under Payne's weight or when Payne slid under the blankets, too. He placed himself behind Rob and wrapped his arms around him, and Rob finally allowed himself to let go. He relaxed, secure in the knowledge that whatever happened, Payne would be there for him.

This was what being mates meant, after all.

Chapter Six

Payne landed on his back. The breath whooshed out of his lungs, but he didn't let that stop him. He scrambled back to his feet, faced Vivian, and circled her.

She grinned and bounced on the balls of her feet. "You're distracted today," she said.

She was right. Payne *was* distracted, and like always lately, it had to do with his mate.

He and Rob had visited Rob's mother a couple more times since her fall. One of those times had been a disaster, but the other had gone well, even though initially, she'd been confused about who Payne was. Even though Payne knew it wasn't her fault, it had hurt a bit. It was the illness, and he'd tried to remember how she'd been that first time.

She'd told Payne to make her son happy and to take care of him, and he had every intention of doing just that for the rest of his life.

That was why he'd been thinking about bonding. He wasn't sure it was something Rob was ready for or that he'd ever want, and he'd avoided talking about it until now, but he wondered if the time had come.

First, he had to kick Vivian's ass.

He moved toward her and saw her get ready for his attack. Instead of throwing himself at her like he'd done before, he quickly shifted and darted between her legs. He'd trained to get out of his clothes quickly and efficiently when he shifted, so he did so without problems. She cried out and turned, looking for him, but he used that moment to go back to where he'd started, quickly shift again, and take her down. He didn't care that he was naked. He wouldn't care that he was naked when he was fighting for the council, either. The only thing that mattered in this kind of fight was to win, and he'd use whatever means he had to use.

This time, it was Vivian who landed on her back. She didn't get back up but stared at the sky. Payne worried that he'd hurt her for a moment, but then she laughed.

"That was great, but can you put your underwear back on?"

Payne rolled his eyes but obeyed.

"Did you really have to get naked?" Vivian asked as she got up.

"I won. Isn't that what matters?"

"I suppose so. You can always flash your opponents and shock them into dying from a heart attack."

"That wasn't a heart attack. That was you hitting the grass."

"He's got you there," Kerwin said from the spot where he'd been sitting and watching the fight.

Vivian narrowed her eyes at him. "Aren't you supposed to be training, too?"

"I'm already a good fighter."

Vivian cracked her knuckles. "Are you? Ready to show me that?"

Kerwin's tail swung as he got up. "Bring it on."

Payne grabbed the rest of his clothes and scrambled out of the way before they could land on him. He moved to the side and put his clothes back on, keeping an eye on what the other two were doing. Kerwin was right when he said that he was a good fighter, but Vivian was better. It didn't take her long to land him on his back, and when she did, she laughed.

"You've been distracted," Seymour said when Payne flopped down next to him.

"I know. I still won."

"Because she wasn't trying to kill you."

Seymour was right. If Payne had been in a real fight, he'd be dead, bleeding out in the grass. He had to be more careful, even though this was only training.

"Want to talk about it?" Seymour asked.

"I want to ask my mate to bond, but I'm afraid I'll send him running."

"Why would you send him running?"

It was hard to explain without giving Seymour too many details. Win had agreed that Greg and Payne could tell the others who they were and where they lived, though, and Payne had been waiting for the right moment to do so. Maybe it had come. It wasn't necessary to tell Seymour about the assassins, but Payne was tired of hiding.

"We're in an odd position," he said.

"Because of the age difference?"

"No."

"Because his mother is ill?"

Payne glared at Seymour. "Are you going to let me speak?"

Seymour mimed locking his lips and throwing away the key. Payne rolled his eyes, but he was glad Seymour was there to listen. He'd become a friend, along with most of the other trainees, and it felt good to have more people in his life.

"Our situation is a bit complicated. Greg and I haven't been allowed to tell you guys about this before, but we've been living with the council assassins for the past four years." Payne paused, giving Seymour the time to wrap his mind around what he'd just said and react.

Seymour gaped. "You mean the real council assassins?"

"Them," Payne confirmed. "They found Greg and me four years ago and rescued us. We didn't have anyone to go back to, and they took us in and finished raising us. Well, Greg was already eighteen, so there wasn't much to raise."

"I'm still stuck on the fact that you've been living with the council assassins. I mean, we're supposed to become them."

"More like we're supposed to become their colleagues. But anyway, that's why Rob moved in with us. He's caring for Jasper, the mate of one of the assassins. Jasper was kidnapped and experimented on, and I guess they tried to turn him into a super-soldier. He has all these new abilities, like strength and speed, and Rob is trying to help him learn how to deal with that."

"That still doesn't tell me why you shouldn't ask Rob to bond with you."

"What happens once he's done with Jasper? He's going to have to go back to his old life, which means that either I'll have to go with him, or he'll have to stay. I don't want him to feel forced to stay with the assassins when he has better things to do, but I don't want to leave them. If we're bonded, one of us won't be able to avoid making changes to his life."

Seymour hummed. "Have you thought that maybe you should talk to him about it?"

"Of course I have. I just think it's not fair to burden him with this when he's already dealing with Jasper and his mother."

"But he's already decided to move in with you guys, right? He had to know that he'd have to stay with you guys for a while in order to help Jasper."

"But he thought that eventually he'd be able to leave."

Seymour groaned. "You have to talk to him about this. Maybe don't lead with the fact that you want to bond with him if you're not sure, but at the very least, ask him what he sees your future looking like. That might give you a hint. I don't see why he wouldn't want to bond with you."

Rob was so smart and good at his job, and Payne didn't want to limit him by forcing him to stay with the assassins. On the other hand, if Payne became an assassin, he'd have to live in secret. He wasn't sure they could mix those things, but strangely, he had faith. Things had been going well between him and Rob. They were mates, and Payne loved Rob. Their differences were still there, and they made Payne feel hesitant, but that didn't mean they couldn't find a way around them. And if they couldn't, well, they'd still be able to make things work. They both wanted to, and in the end, that was all that mattered. They were ready to try and make sacrifices.

"What are you two doing?" Hawthorne asked from behind them, making both of them jump.

Payne tilted his head back to look at the trainer. Hawthorne was looking down at him with a scowl.

"Do you want a cup of tea?" he asked. "Some cookies, maybe?"

Payne scrambled to his feet. "Sorry."

"Get back to work."

They did. Payne wasn't sure he had answers to his questions, but Seymour wouldn't be the one who'd give them to him anyway. No, for that, he'd have to talk to Rob, and even though it terrified him, he was going to do it. He had to in order for them to take the next step in their relationship. Besides, what were the odds that Rob would tell him he didn't want him anymore?

Payne prayed they were zero.

Rob smiled when the kitchen door opened and Greg and Payne appeared. He'd expected them to come straight to the kitchen once they were home, like always. He had no idea what they did exactly in their program, but he knew it was partly physical and that they were always starving by the time they were done. So instead of waiting for Payne to come to him once he'd eaten, he'd come to Payne and waited for him with a snack ready.

Payne walked in, and his eyes widened when he saw that Rob was there. "You're not in the infirmary," he said as he sauntered close and kissed Rob's cheek.

Rob's entire face flushed and he looked around, but no one cared that his mate was kissing him. "I knew you'd be hungry, so I thought I'd get something ready." He pushed the plate containing the sandwich he'd made toward Payne.

Payne's smile widened, and he flopped into the seat next to Rob. Rob always struggled to sit on the stools around the kitchen island, but Payne made it look effortless. Most of the people who lived here made it look effortless. This was a Rob problem, and he was very much aware of it. He was as graceful as a drunk hippopotamus out of water.

Payne pulled the sandwich closer and made to take a bite, but Graham stopped him before he could. "Wash your hands."

"I washed them before leaving the training facility," Payne protested.

Graham's eyes narrowed. "I don't know if I should believe you."

"I'm not sixteen anymore, Graham."

Graham stared at Payne for a moment longer before nodding. "Sorry. Sometimes, it's hard to remember."

Payne grinned and finally took a bite of the sandwich. It was the only thing Rob could make, and he hoped it was decent. Graham had offered to get something ready for Payne and Greg, but he was already cooking dinner, and besides, Rob wanted to be able to take care of his mate. It was just a sandwich, for fuck's sake.

Greg was eating, too, on the other side of the counter. His mate was present, silent as ever, and Rob wasn't quite sure how to behave. He knew how close Payne and Greg were, and he wondered if that meant he should become Evan's friend. He didn't see that happening, both because of how silent

Evan was and because of how awkward Rob was.

Greg chatted about his day to Evan, telling him what had happened and how it had gone, but Payne was unusually silent next to Rob. Rob gave him a moment, thinking that maybe he was just focused on eating, but it was unlike Payne not to ask Rob how his day had gone at the very least.

Rob cleared his throat. "How was your day?" he asked. Payne was usually the one to ask that question, but Rob could do it as well as he did.

"It was fine," Payne said.

Rob blinked. "Just fine?"

"Yeah. I mean, we've been doing the same things day in and day out. It's kind of the point to learn them, you know? I don't want to bother you by telling you yet again that I trained and kicked ass."

This was *definitely* not like Payne—something was wrong. He didn't want everyone to be aware of that, so he leaned closer. "What happened?"

"Nothing happened," Payne answered too quickly, and he was clearly avoiding looking at Rob now.

Rob bit his lower lip. What was he supposed to do? He didn't want to force Payne to talk to him, especially if Payne didn't want to, but he was worried. He could tell something had happened, and he wanted to be there for Payne, but how could he when Payne wouldn't talk to him?

"Are you sure?" he asked.

Payne smiled, but it was a little forced. "I'm sure. How was your day, then?"

Rob supposed he'd allow Payne to distract him, at least for now. They were in public, so it wasn't the right time to ask Payne for an explanation. Besides, maybe Payne didn't want to give him one. Rob had no idea what he was doing, and he was afraid that pushing too hard would trigger a fight. They hadn't fought yet, and while he knew that eventually it would happen because it was what happened in relationships, it broke his heart just to think about it. He never wanted Payne to be angry at him. He never wanted Payne to feel like he needed to hide things from him.

What was happening?

"Rob?" Payne asked.

Rob shook himself and forced a smile. It clearly didn't work, because Payne frowned, but before he could ask what was wrong, Rob started telling him about his day. Like always when he was nervous, he went into a lot of details Payne didn't care about and probably didn't understand. Not that Payne said anything about it. He kept on eating, and he was smiling. Rob could almost believe he was interested in what he was saying, which was a step further than any of his exes had ever gone. They hadn't hesitated to tell Rob they didn't care about his work. Payne would never do anything like that, and it was one of the reasons Rob loved him.

But now he wondered. He'd gone into this relationship expecting Payne to get annoyed at him eventually and possibly break up with him. Mates didn't have to be together just because they shared a bond. He'd always thought it would be better for Payne to find someone else, both because of their age difference and because of the kind of person Rob was, but Payne had dismissed that. Maybe he'd finally realized that Rob was right after all. Maybe he'd met someone at this training facility, and he was trying to find a way to gently dump Rob.

Rob's mouth was dry, but he continued talking, even though he barely remembered what he was saying. Was that what was about to happen? Was Payne going to break up with him? It felt like a distinct possibility, and he didn't know how to deal with it, or even if he could. He'd allowed himself to hope that he and Payne were really doing this, and now, he wondered.

Was he about to lose his mate?

By the time Payne was done eating, Graham had looked like he was sleeping with his eyes open. He'd been listening to what Rob was saying, but his eyes had glazed over. At least he wasn't doing anything he had to focus on too hard, since he was cutting vegetables for a salad. Rob felt shame crawl up his back. He should have shut up, but he'd been unable to. He knew how he was when he was nervous, and he had to learn to deal with it instead of throwing an info dump at the people listening to him.

"The sandwich was good," Payne said.

Rob found himself smiling despite his feelings. "It's pretty much the only thing I can put together, so I'm glad you liked it."

Payne nodded and got to his feet. He stretched, and Rob found himself unable to look away. In moments like this, he was still amazed that Payne had chosen him. It would have been much easier for him to walk away, but he was here, by Rob's side.

For how long?

"I really need a shower," Payne said. "I should have grabbed one before coming to eat, but I was starving."

"All right," Rob said. He wasn't sure what Payne expected from him.

Payne stared at him for a moment before frowning. "In case you didn't realize, I was asking if you wanted to come upstairs with me."

"You didn't say those words."

"I didn't realize I had to say them. Do you want to come upstairs with me, though?"

Rob got up from the stool so fast that he almost fell on his face. Graham muffled a laugh, but Rob wouldn't have cared if he'd laughed in his face. He knew he was a mess. He wasn't offended by people laughing at him, especially when he considered them friends.

"I'll come with you," he said. He didn't know why Payne was asking him if he wanted to be in his room while he showered, but he supposed he was about to find out.

Unless Payne just wanted to get him alone. Maybe he was taking pity on Rob and about to tell him it was better if they stopped seeing each other when they were alone, so that Rob would be able to spend the rest of the evening on his own licking his wounds. Payne wouldn't do that in front of the others because it wasn't the kind of person he was, but Rob's mouth went dry at the thought.

He waited for Payne to say goodbye to Greg and Evan, then the two of them headed out of the kitchen and toward the stairs. They were silent until they reached Payne's bedroom, but Rob couldn't stand it anymore once they were there. As soon as the door was closed behind him, he turned to Payne, who was already taking off his t-shirt.

"I'm going to shower," Payne said at the exact same time Rob asked, "Are you about to break up with me?"

This wasn't going the way Payne had expected it to go. Rob had noticed something was up with him, and he was staring at him with wide, slightly wild eyes.

"Of course I'm not breaking up with you," Payne said. "Why would you think that?"

"Because of the way you're behaving. Something's wrong with you, and you won't tell me what it is. That means that whatever's wrong has to do with me, and considering my past relationships, the most probable explanation is that you're fed up with me and want to break up."

That was the last thing Payne wanted Rob to think. He dropped his t-shirt and stepped closer to his mate, catching Rob's waist and pulling him close. "I'm not breaking up with you."

Rob was clearly skeptical. "Aren't you? Because I wouldn't blame you if you did. I know I'm a lot and that not everyone wants to have to deal with me."

If Payne ever met Rob's exes, he'd tear them apart with his bare hands. They'd done a number on Rob, and now he believed it was impossible for anyone to want to be with him. It hurt Payne to know that, but he wasn't sure how to help. Maybe repeating time and time again that he wasn't going anywhere would help.

What also would help was if he didn't act like an idiot and like something was wrong, especially when nothing was. Yes, he was nervous because he was about to ask Rob if he wanted them to bond, but that didn't mean he had to freak Rob out over that.

"I promise you that I'm not about to break up with you," he said. "But I am worried about something." There was no way he could hide that. Rob already knew.

Rob's eyes had narrowed, and he stared at Payne. "Does that something have to do with me?"

"Most of my life has to do with you. You're my mate. You're central to my existence and my thoughts."

Like always when Payne said something like that, Rob got all flustered. He looked away and his cheeks went pink, and while it was adorable, Payne didn't say that out loud. He didn't want Rob to think he didn't take him seriously.

It would be impossible for him not to. There was no one as serious as Rob, and Payne liked that. There was a reason Rob was his mate, and Payne thought that it was because Rob was the kind of person Payne wanted to be with. He was serious, quiet most of the time, but passionate. What he did was important for many people, not just Jasper. He also understood why Payne wanted to be a council assassin. Payne had expected that to be a problem between them, but it had never been. Rob had accepted that was what Payne would do once he was done with training, and that was that.

"So you're not going to break up with me," Rob said.

"I promise you that I'm not. Just give me a little time to wrap my mind around what's going on, all right?"

Rob was still hesitant, but Payne wasn't sure what else to say to him. He wanted to talk about them bonding, but he needed to put his words together instead of blurting them out and hoping Rob would understand. He wasn't sure if Rob had thought about them bonding, and if he had, how he felt about it. The thought that Payne might ask him to bond and Rob might say no was terrifying, which was one more reason Payne needed some time.

He kissed Rob's forehead, then headed to the bathroom. Rob didn't try to stop him, but he was still tense, so much so that Payne could have sworn he could feel him vibrate behind him. He wanted to reassure him again, but instead, he walked into the bathroom and closed the door behind himself. Once there, he took a deep breath and waited a few seconds to gather his thoughts.

It was normal to be afraid that Rob would reject him, but he shouldn't be. Even if Rob said he wasn't ready to bond, it didn't change the fact that they were together. They were mates, and eventually, they *would* bond. Payne was sure of that. It didn't matter that it happened now, in a week, a month, or next year. As long as he and Rob were together, it would happen.

Knowing that helped, and Payne quickly undressed. He turned on the water in the shower, waited until it warmed, then stepped under it. He closed his eyes and tilted his head up, finally allowing himself to relax. Yes, he was nervous, but he and Rob would still be together no matter what happened. They'd been working for their relationship, and while there were still a few kinks to work through, they were doing well.

Payne couldn't imagine his life without Rob in it, and he was pretty sure the same went for Rob.

From what Payne had noticed, Rob didn't actually need to work with Jasper most of the time. He had in the beginning, but now he'd done all the tests he wanted to do on Jasper, which meant that he could head back home and work from there if he wanted. Instead, he'd stuck around, and Payne knew it was partly because of him. Rob wanted to be close, and Payne wanted him to be. They were both finding a way to make things work with the other, finding out what they were ready to compromise on and what they weren't, and he liked it.

He just wished their relationship didn't come with the deep terror that Rob would realize he was so much better than Payne one day.

He took his time in the shower, but he couldn't hide there forever. Eventually, he had to turn off the water and dry off. Once he did, he realized he hadn't brought any clean clothes in the bathroom, which meant he had to face Rob mostly naked. He didn't care, but Rob was still hesitant about being naked with him. Considering what Payne knew about Rob's exes, it made sense, and once again, it made him want to find them and strangle them.

He wrapped his towel around his waist and left the bathroom, even though it felt like a safe haven. He half expected Rob to have taken out his phone and to be working, but instead, Rob was sitting at the foot of Payne's bed, wringing his fingers together. He was also bouncing one knee, and both these things were sure signs that he was nervous. Apparently, even though Payne had tried to reassure him, he still thought something was wrong.

Payne sighed, and just then, Rob looked up. His eyes widened and he shot to his feet, gesturing toward the door. "I should probably go. You need some rest before dinner."

"Sit down," Payne said.

Rob sat without arguing. He stared at Payne with wide eyes, and Payne went to his dresser to grab a pair of shorts. Without looking back at Rob, he dropped his towel, then stepped into the shorts. He didn't miss the strangled sound Rob made, and it made him feel a little smug, but they weren't here to have sex.

Not yet, anyway.

Payne went to sit next to Rob. He grabbed Rob's knee so Rob had to stop bouncing it, but Rob started moving his other knee instead. That made Payne smile, but he didn't want Rob to be nervous for longer than necessary.

"I'm not breaking up with you," he repeated. "In fact, it's the opposite."

Rob swallowed loudly. "What do you mean?"

"That I've been thinking. I'm in love with you, Rob. I realize it happened fast, but how could I not be?"

Rob nodded, his expression grim. "Because of the bond."

"How I feel about you doesn't have anything to do with the bond. It has everything to do with you being a smart, sweet, lovely man."

Rob blinked. "I don't think anyone has ever described me that way."

"Then they were idiots. That's who you are, and I'm in love with you. I never want us to be separated." Payne swallowed. If they were going to talk about this, he needed to be completely honest. "But just like you don't understand why I feel the way I do, I'm still not sure why you want to be with me. You could have so much better. I'm young, have no idea what you're talking about most of the time, and sometimes, I wonder if fate made a mistake, not because you're not good enough for me, but rather because you're *too* good for me."

Payne looked away. He knew what he thought Rob's answer would be and what he hoped it would be. He couldn't truly believe that just like he wanted to be with Rob, Rob wanted to be with him. Asking Rob to bond was as much to reassure himself as it would be to reassure Rob, but he didn't know how to say the words.

He was *terrified* to say them, and now that he had the opportunity to do so, they were stuck at the back of his throat, unable to come out.

That was going to be a problem.

Rob never wanted Payne to feel like he wasn't good enough, dammit. Had he done or said anything that pointed that way? He couldn't remember, but he hoped that wasn't the case.

Was that what had been on Payne's mind? Was he afraid that Rob was going to break up with him, just like Rob was terrified that Payne would break up with him?

They sucked at this relationship thing. They were supposed to talk and reassure each other, not obsess over a potential breakup that would probably never come.

Rob put his hand on top of the one Payne still had on his knee. He forced himself to still his other knee, sucked in a breath, and tried to explain what he was thinking without making a mess of it.

"I couldn't have wanted a better mate than you," he said slowly. When he rushed his words, he tended to say stupid things. He wanted Payne to understand how important he was to him, though, and clearly, he hadn't done a great job until now.

"Yeah?" Payne sounded hesitant.

"Of course. I understand where you're coming from because I feel the same, so how about we promise each other that we'll talk about it whenever we feel like we're not good enough? Because you're more than good enough for me, Payne. It doesn't matter how old you are. You're thoughtful and caring, passionate, and strong. You're everything I could have wanted from a mate, even when I didn't think I'd ever have one."

Payne stared at him for a moment. Rob held his breath, wondering what his mate was about to say. Whatever it was could make or break Rob's happiness, and knowing that he depended on Payne so much was petrifying. He couldn't imagine what his life would be without Payne now, even though until recently, he hadn't known his mate.

But now, he did, and he never wanted to lose him.

"Bond with me," Payne blurted out.

Rob blinked. "I'm sorry?"

Payne slid his hand out from under Rob's and rubbed his face. "I'm sorry. I wanted to ask differently, but I think it would help both of us with the way we feel. You were thinking I wanted to break up with you, and I often wonder if it would be better for you to do the same. Maybe if we're bonded, we'll finally be able to accept that we're in each other's lives to stay."

Rob couldn't say he hadn't thought about bonding. He had. He just hadn't believed it would happen anytime soon. "We haven't known each other long," he said slowly.

"Do we need to? Because I already know you're everything to me. I already know I don't want to be without you, ever. I already know I love you and that you're it for me. Even if something were to happen, I wouldn't be able to move on."

Rob hoped that wasn't true. Even if something happened to him, he wanted Payne to be happy eventually. Not that he was planning on anything happening to him, but he was older. If he and Payne bonded, his aging would slow down. He'd still be older, but he'd have decades to be happy with Payne. "All right," he said.

Payne stared at him as if he hadn't heard him. "All right?"

"Yes. Or did you want me to say no?"

Payne grabbed one of Rob's hands and squeezed. "I just thought you'd have to think about it, maybe make a list of pros and cons."

It wasn't a surprise that Payne already knew Rob so well. "I already did."

"Yeah?"

Rob nodded. "I knew that this conversation would come up eventually. I wanted to be ready when it did, so I made a list."

A smile finally appeared on Payne's lips. "Do I want to know what was in the cons list?"

"It was nothing we haven't already discussed."

"So now you only have pros?"

"How could I not? I want to bond with you." Rob was slightly worried that they were doing it for the wrong reason, but was there a wrong reason to bond? He and Payne wanted to be together. They both had their hang-ups, and bonding would help them with that. In the end, wasn't that what mattered?

Payne laughed, and his expression finally relaxed. Now he truly looked like a twenty-year-old man who didn't have a worry in the world, and Rob wanted things to stay that way. He wanted to be there for his mate for the rest of their lives. Bonding with Payne would allow him to do that, and hopefully, it would mean that Payne would never again think that he wasn't good enough for Rob.

Payne threw himself at Rob. Rob squeaked, not having expected it, and they both fell to the bed. Before Rob could say anything, Payne's lips were on him, and he was more than happy to kiss Payne back.

They tugged at each other's clothes, frantic to get the other naked. Rob had no idea what was going on, but he was on board with whatever Payne wanted.

In theory, he knew how bonding worked. Payne would

have to bite him, probably on the neck, and drink his blood. He'd also have to cut himself so that Rob could drink his, and once they both had drunk enough blood, the bond would snap into place.

That was in theory. In practice, they'd have to find out what worked and what didn't work, and that was something only they could do. It was personal, and while Rob couldn't wait to be bonded to Payne, he was also nervous.

But knowing he was doing this with Payne helped. Knowing that Payne saw him as a beautiful man he'd fallen in love with also did, so when Payne quickly opened the buttons of Rob's shirt, Rob didn't protest.

They'd been naked together before, but Rob had always felt awkward. He still did, but this time especially, it was easy to forget how self-conscious he was. It was easy to focus on what was about to happen between them and only that. Payne didn't care what Rob looked like. He didn't care that Rob was too thin, that he forgot to eat, and that he was a mess. They were making things work, even though Rob had never thought they'd be able to.

He should have had more faith in Payne.

Payne made a victorious sound once he had all the buttons of Rob's shirt open. He pushed it off Rob's shoulders, and Rob pulled himself up into a half-sitting position so he could throw it on the floor. By the time he stretched out on his back again, Payne had unbuttoned his slacks and was sliding them down his legs. He'd left Rob's underwear on, but Rob pushed them off his hips. Payne grinned at him and helped him with them, too. He had to stop for a moment to take off Rob's shoes and socks, and then it only took seconds for Rob to be naked.

Payne was still wearing his shorts, but it was easy to get rid of them as well. Rob expected Payne to drop on top of him once they were both naked, but instead, he moved toward his nightstand.

Rob's mouth went dry. They were really doing this, and while he was nervous, there was no sign of the fear he'd been sure would be there. Whatever happened, whatever stupid thing he said or did, Payne wouldn't care.

Payne held up a bottle of lube. "We don't have to do anything that involves penetration, but I thought I'd put it on the table."

Rob had never tried to be seductive with Payne. The few times he'd attempted to do it with his exes, they'd laughed at him. It still stung, but he knew Payne, and he trusted him. Payne wouldn't laugh, and he wouldn't make fun of him.

So Rob opened his legs. He exposed himself, made himself vulnerable, and once again, Payne caught him. He smiled softly, but there was a warmth in his gaze, and when he raked his gaze up and down Rob's body, it was almost as if he was touching him. He wanted Rob just as much as Rob wanted him.

Payne crawled between Rob's legs, then finally lowered himself on top of him. "We don't have to do anything you're not comfortable with," he murmured, but he was already opening the lube.

"I want to do it with you. I trust you."

Payne nodded. "But if you're not comfortable with me making love to you, you could make love to me."

Rob's mouth went dry. "I'll want to try that eventually, but not now." Now he wanted to give himself up entirely in a way he'd never been able to. Payne was the only man he could ever trust with something like this, and not for the first time, Rob silently thanked whoever had given him Payne.

Payne didn't protest, and he didn't try to change Rob's mind. Instead, he leaned slightly to the side, just enough to be able to push a hand between their bodies. Rob's breath hitched when he felt Payne's slick fingers on his stomach, then on his hip, then the inside of his thigh. Payne wasn't going to be quick about it, and Rob loved it. He wanted them to make the most out of this moment, because they'd only bond once, and this was it.

For once, Rob managed to push away the thoughts as he allowed Payne to take care of him. He didn't obsess over whether or not Payne liked what he was seeing and doing. He didn't wonder what Payne was thinking. He didn't doubt that Payne wanted him because it was impossible to with how hard Payne's cock was.

And once Payne was done prepping him, he didn't hesitate to open both his legs and arms to him. He welcomed him into his body, and it felt right for the first time ever. He fully trusted the man he was with, and he knew that whatever happened, they'd be together forever.

He almost cried. He was overwhelmed, and while it would have been easy to lose himself in the pleasure of having Payne inside of him, he didn't. He wanted to be aware of every single second between them.

He knew the next step, so he caught Payne's gaze with his, then slowly tilted his head to the side. Payne's eyes were already wide, as if he couldn't quite believe what he was doing, but they went round as he focused on Rob's exposed neck. For just a second, Rob wondered if maybe he'd been too brash. He didn't have more than one second to wonder, though, because then Payne buried his face against his neck and bit him.

He didn't ask Rob if he was sure. He didn't hesitate. He just bit Rob, and while there was some pain, it soon settled into a steady throb that drove Rob nuts. He could have sworn he felt it in his groin as well as in his neck, even though it wasn't physically possible.

The rhythm of Payne's thrusts into him faltered, and Rob clung to him. For a moment, he didn't understand what Payne was doing when he reached for his own neck. Payne didn't even look up or lean back from Rob's neck. He just slashed into his neck, and blood beaded on the cut. For a second, Rob stared at it. If he drank the blood, there would be no going back.

Good.

Rob latched onto the wound and sucked. He wrinkled his nose because blood tasted like, well, blood. It wasn't pleasurable, but it was the only thing in this situation that wasn't. As soon as he started sucking, Payne fucked into him harder and faster. It was as if he'd been waiting for Rob to do this, for them to be completing the bond together.

Rob didn't know how long he sucked down Payne's blood, but he knew the exact moment in which they became one. Something snapped into place, and he finally felt complete in a way he never had. He cried out, letting go of Payne's neck, but it didn't matter, because the bond was complete.

It was overwhelming in a way Rob hadn't expected. He could feel Payne's emotions, what he was going through, and it mirrored so closely what Rob felt that it was almost an echo of it. Just like Rob, Payne loved. He lusted, he strained toward his orgasm, and more deeply, he was at peace and satisfied. He'd found his place in the world, and no matter how hard it was to understand, that place was in Rob's arms.

Rob wasn't sure what happened, but he bit down on the wound on Payne's neck. Payne shouted and slammed into Rob just as Rob came. Rob couldn't tell where his orgasm ended and where Payne's started, but he didn't think it mattered.

Nothing but Payne mattered, and it wasn't a feeling Rob was used to. Maybe it wouldn't be so hard to dedicate as much time to Payne as Payne deserved, after all. Maybe Rob would finally be able to do Payne justice and stop obsessing over his work. He wouldn't have done it for anyone but Payne, but he'd even quit his job entirely for his mate. The fact that Payne would never ask him to do so made him the perfect man for Rob, and Rob promised himself that he'd do everything he could to make Payne happy.

Forever.

CHAPTER SEVEN

Payne caught the punch aimed at his face, twisted his hold on Kerwin's fist, and moved sideways. He pushed, giving more force to Kerwin's movement. Kerwin stumbled forward, and Payne let go. At the same time, he raised his foot and pressed it to Kerwin's ass, pushing him forward.

It should have worked, but Payne hadn't considered Kerwin's tail. Instead of Kerwin tilting forward and falling on his face, Kerwin's tail wrapped around Payne's leg, keeping him where he was. Kerwin turned, a wide smile on his lips.

"Good!" Jamison said, clapping his hands from where he was watching their fight. "Payne, you have to keep in mind that not everyone is human."

Payne grinned. He never looked away from Kerwin, and he saw the exact moment when Kerwin decided to throw himself at him and see what happened. If Payne stayed where he was, they'd have collided.

Instead, Payne shifted.

"Not fair!" Kerwin yelled.

Payne scrambled out of his clothes, then ran a wide circle around Kerwin. The demon tried to catch him with his hands and his tail, but Payne was too fast for him. He ran and ran, tiring Kerwin out, but the demon never gave up. So once he was sure Kerwin was tired, Payne went around him and jumped up. He put all his strength into his paws, and even though he was tiny in his fennec fox form, it was enough to make Kerwin tilt forward.

There was nothing for Kerwin to grab onto this time, and

just like Payne had been planning, he fell flat on his face.

Jamison clapped his hands again. "Good. Kerwin, just like Payne had to remember that not everyone is human, you should, too. You rely too much on your tail when you fight, and it's not always a good thing."

Kerwin rolled to his back. Payne trotted to him, paused by his face, and swiped his tongue down Kerwin's cheek. Kerwin yelped and scrubbed his cheek, glaring at Payne. "That's disgusting," he said. "Why don't you go lick your mate?"

Payne would have told him that was what he'd rather do, too, if he'd had a human mouth. Instead, he stuck his tongue out and lolled it to the side.

Kerwin laughed. "I wasn't kidding." He pointed at something behind Payne.

Payne turned. He was stunned to find Rob hovering a few feet away, watching him. He stood next to Hawthorne, which probably explained why he looked like he wanted nothing more than to run away.

That was how Payne felt most of the time when he had to deal with the trainer.

Payne gave Kerwin's cheek one last lick. He ignored Kerwin's protest and made his way to his mate. He stopped in front of him and grinned, exposing his fangs, relieved when Rob visibly relaxed.

Hawthorne rolled his eyes. "You did good," he said gruffly. "Now, stop staring at your mate and grab your clothes. It's time for lunch."

Hawthorne stepped away, but Rob crouched in front of Payne. He reached out and gently scratched under Payne's chin, and Payne tilted his head to give him better access. He loved when his mate petted him, whether in his human form or in his fox one.

He didn't let Rob do it for too long, though. He was too curious why Rob was here. He'd expressed some interest in watching Payne train, but he'd never come, no matter how many times Payne told him it would be okay.

But today, he was here, and Payne wanted to know what was happening. So he quickly shifted, ignored the way Rob was staring at his body, and put his clothes back on.

"What are you doing here?" he asked as he looped an arm around Rob's waist to pull him closer.

Rob resisted. For one second, Payne worried he'd done something Rob didn't want. Then he noticed that Rob was looking around, almost as if he was afraid someone would see them.

Someone definitely would, since half the people Payne trained with were staring at them with open curiosity.

"I was just curious," Rob said softly. "The way you talk about this place made me want to see it."

"I'm glad you came."

Rob nodded, but he continued looking around. "Maybe it would be better to put more space between us?"

Payne didn't let that offend him because he knew why Rob was saying it. "They won't say anything. They already know everything they need to know about you."

"Which is?"

"That you're my mate and that I love you."

"I just don't want them to judge you for the age difference or other things."

"They know you're older than me. You think Seymour didn't blurt out everything he found out about you as soon as he came back?"

Seymour was the only one except for Greg who'd ever met Rob, but everyone knew about Rob. Unfortunately, Seymour had told Kerwin about Payne's mate as soon as he'd come back from the home where Rob's mother was, and by the time Payne had come back to training the next day, everyone knew that Payne's mate was a hot, older nerd. Payne had never told

Rob about it because he knew how embarrassed Rob would be, but he was proud to be with Rob, and he didn't care who saw them together.

He kissed Rob's cheek. "I promise they don't have anything to say about you and I being together. Besides, I want them to see us together. I want to brag about you being mine."

Rob leaned against Payne and sighed. "Do you?"

"How could I not want to brag? I have the most handsome man here in my arms."

Just like Payne expected, Rob's cheeks turned red. He glared at Payne, but there was no heat behind it. "Everyone here is handsome, from the trainees to the trainers. I don't know how you can say that I'm the most handsome."

"I can say it because it's the truth, at least to me. Now, are you here to watch me train, or can you stay for lunch?"

Rob hesitated. "Does this mean I'll have lunch with all your friends?"

"We usually have lunch together, so probably. You can sit between Greg and me, if you'd feel more comfortable."

Payne was only half surprised when Rob nodded. Rob was making a lot of effort to be part of Payne's life and make him feel like he mattered, which was probably one of the reasons he was here. He kept apologizing for how much time he spent working, no matter how many times Payne told him it didn't matter.

It truly didn't. Payne had always known how important Rob's job was to him and the people he helped and that sometimes, he'd come second. He was fine with that as long as he became first again once the work was over. Sometimes it was still hard for Rob to do that, but his presence here showed that he was getting better.

Payne grabbed Rob's hand and pulled him toward the others. Kerwin was so eager to meet him that he was bouncing on the balls of his feet, and Payne glared at him, hoping he'd understand he had to tone it down. Even if he did so, this would still be overwhelming for Rob.

That was why Payne kept an eye on him to make sure he was okay. He didn't seem to know what to say to the others, but that was fine because Kerwin took charge. He introduced Rob to everyone, and every time he mentioned that Rob was Payne's mate, Payne's chest puffed up without him meaning it to. He was proud to have Rob as his mate, and that was never going to change.

"It's a lot of people," Rob murmured as they followed the others toward the cafeteria.

"You don't have to remember all their names right away," Payne promised.

"I want to. They're important to you, which means they're important to me."

Payne's heart felt like it expanded, and his chest was too tight for it. "I love you," he said.

Rob looked startled, but he nodded. "I love you, too."

And in the end, that was all that mattered. Payne wished he could find whoever had decided that Rob would be his mate to thank them, but since he couldn't, he promised himself he'd take good care of his mate. It was the least Rob deserved and everything Payne had ever wanted.

With Rob, Payne's life was complete. He had his friends and his family, a home, and the best job he could ever have wanted.

And he had love.

ABOUT THE AUTHOR

Catherine is the creator of several series, most of them paranormal, including the Whitedell Pride Series and the Gillham Pack Series. While she graduated in translation, she decided to go the writer's way because it was more fun to create her own stories and characters.

She's been living in Italy for more than twenty years, but she's a daughter of the North—Belgium to be precise—and she misses it so much that she's already planning to move back.

She loves pizza—probably too much—her son, her pets, and of course, books. She sneaks some reading time into her schedule every time she has five minutes free from writing, demands from her various pets and son, and lastly, housework.

Connect with her:

lievens.catherine@gmail.com
BookBub: https://www.bookbub.com/authors/catherine-lievens
Website: https://authorcatherinelievens.com/
Facebook: https://www.facebook.com/catherine.lievens.9
Facebook Group: https://www.facebook.com/groups/411788002341528/
Twitter: https://twitter.com/authorCLievens
Newsletter: http://eepurl.com/c-uvKn